The Babysitters Club Special

SEA CITY, HERE WE COME!

It was hard to stay in a good mood at the BSC meeting. There was Shannon, on the way to stardom at summer camp. Jessi, Mal and Stacey were a day away from fun and sun. Mary Anne and Dawn were all starry-eyed about mini-camp. And Kristy was her usual gung-ho self about the Krushers.

Thank goodness I was going to Sea City. I kept thinking about that. Every time I imagined Jessi or Stacey or Mal on the beach, I just imagined myself there, with them.

Only eight days and counting! I could practically feel the ocean breezes.

Hurray! Summer's finally here and the Babysitters are *all* on holiday in Sea City – even Logan Bruno! Everyone's having *such* a good time. Mary Anne showing Logan the sights, Mallory falling in love, and Jessi, busy being "super-sitter". But nobody bargained on Hurricane Bill – heading *straight* for Sea City. Uh-oh!

Scholastic Children's Books,
Scholastic Publications Ltd,
7–9 Pratt Street, London NW1 0AE, UK

Scholastic Inc.,
555 Broadway, New York, NY 10012-3999, USA

Scholastic Canada Ltd,
123 Newkirk Road, Richmond Hill,
Ontario, Canada L4C 3G5

Ashton Scholastic Pty Ltd,
P O Box 579, Gosford, New South Wales,
Australia

Ashton Scholastic Ltd,
Private Bag 92801, Penrose, Auckland,
New Zealand

First published in the US by Scholastic Inc., 1993
First published in the UK by Scholastic Children's Books, 1994

Text copyright © Ann M. Martin, 1993

ISBN 0 590 55662 2

THE BABY-SITTERS CLUB is a trademark of Scholastic Inc.

Typeset in Plantin by Contour Typesetters, Southall, London
Printed by Cox & Wyman Ltd, Reading, Berks

SEA CITY, HERE WE COME!

Ann M. Martin

Hippo

The author gratefully acknowledges
Peter Lerangis
for his help in
preparing this manuscript.

Dear Keisha,

Guess what? I'm going to the Jersey shore for the first two weeks in August! I got a job taking care of the Pike kids with Mallory. They have this holiday house in Sea City, and it's right on the beach. Like, step out the front door and into the sand!

They were thinking of taking one of the older babysitters, but Mal convinced them to let me go. I am going to be the best sitter they ever dreamed of!

Love,
Your best cousin,
Jessi

Mary Anne,

Hi! Sorry I haven't written lately. Baseball season was a killer. I hurt my finger throwing a curve ball, so I spent the first week of summer holiday soaking it in pickle brine. (My finger, not the ball.) Anyway, enough said about your favourite sport. (Ha.ha.)

What's up? Are you going to Sea City this summer? I am! I'm going to be a mother's helper. Toby's going to be there, too.

Write back, okay? Hope I see you at the beach!

Your friend,
Alex

P.S. Is Stacey going to Sea City? Toby wants to know.

Deer Kristy
Were on holiday alredy. So Linnie and I cant come to Crushers practis this summer. Because dad had to take off earlier. I yeled and cried but it didnt matter. Linny's pretty angry.

From,
Hannie

2

Dear Dad,

How's July in the Big Apple? Catching any rays on the way to the E train? Just kidding! But next time I C U I'll be BRONZE! (I hope.) Mrs Barrett's renting a house in Sea City near the Pikes, and she asked me if I could go along to help take care of her kids. I said, "Twist my arm!" No, really, I told her I'd ask permish. Mum says OK. Do you, too? (You do, right?)

Can't wait to hear.

LUV,
Stacey

STONEYBROOK PUBLIC SCHOOLS
STONEYBROOK MIDDLE SCHOOL
ELM STREET
STONEYBROOK, CT

Dear   Ms Kishi
We are looking forward to seeing you at summer school.

Please report to room Gym at the high school, at 9:00 a.m. on Monday, July 1.

Sincerely,
Benjamin Taylor
Principal

3

Hi, Dad! Hi, Jeff!

Can't wait to see you at the end of Aug. I will have SO much to tell you by then. Here's why. This month, Mary Anne and I are going to run a summer Mini-Camp for the neighbourhood kids! Now for the great news. The Pikes have invited Kristy, Claudia, Mary Anne, and ME to their beach house for one whole week in August! Yea! And Jessi, Mal, and Stacey will already be there. SEA CITY, HERE WE COME!

Oh. Can you think of a better name for our Mini-Camp? Richard suggested "Club Mad" (for _Mary Anne_ and _Dawn_), but we said NO WAY! Anyway, eight kids have signed up already.

Save some CA sun for me!

Kisses & hugs,
Dawn

Dearest Stacey,

Have a fabulous time at the beach. Just make sure to bring back some saltwater toffee for your old man.

Love,
Hot, sweltering Dad

1st CHAPTER

Kristy

Friday

Dear Aunt Colleen & Uncle Wallace,

What a busy July! Krushers' summer season is already almost over. (Whew!) Also, the BSC had its last <u>full</u> meeting today. Three members are going on holiday tomorrow. The rest of us are going in a week. So the next postcard you get from me will be from... Sea City! I am totally psyched. Say hi to Ashley, Berk, Grace, & Peter!

XXX OOO
Kristy

"Sweet," Claudia Kishi said. "With a mild crunch and kind of a nutty aftertaste."

Jessi Ramsey nodded. "It gets nice and crumbly in your mouth. But it doesn't have the same . . . *burst* of flavour."

"The ingredients are definitely inferior," Logan Bruno added.

We sat, chewing thoughtfully, saying nothing. We looked like nine cows grazing in pasture.

"Okay, let's vote," Claudia said. "All those in favour of Sample A, raise your hands. . . . Sample B?"

No, we were not having some gourmet food sampling. It was minutes before our Friday Babysitters Club meeting, and Claudia was conducting an End-of-the-Season Junk Food Blindfold Taste-test. We were to decide which tasted better, Heath Bars or Skor Bars. She had bought several of each and removed the wrappers so we wouldn't know which we were eating.

Strange, huh? That's Claudia. She's the BSC's resident junk food addict. Her bedroom (our official headquarters) is crammed full of chocolate, crisps, and sweets. And it's all well hidden, because her parents are firm believers in Good Nutrition. (They're also believers in Good Literature, which is why Claudia has also hidden her Nancy Drew books amongst her socks and underwear.)

Claud is a talented artist, sculptor, and

7

jewellery-maker. Mr and Mrs Kishi approve of those things, so Claud keeps her art materials in full view. Which is how she prevents her parents from finding her hidden stuff. She tells them no one's allowed to touch her works in progress— which occupy every corner of the room.

You can probably picture the place. It's a pigsty. (Sorry, but it is.) Us BSCers put up with it, though. One, because we love Claud. And two, because she's the only one of us who has her own private phone with a private phone number. (The phone is crucial to the success of our business.)

Here's how our club works. We meet on Monday, Wednesday, and Friday afternoons from 5:30 to 6:00. During those times, we take calls from neighbourhood parents who need sitters. We have seven members (nine, if you count our associates). So our clients know they can book a reliable, expert sitter with just one call.

The BSC was an idea waiting to happen. (I read that expression somewhere, and it really fits.) Actually, it was *my* idea. I thought of it a while ago when my mum was having trouble arranging a sitter. And it has really worked. Now we have tons of regular clients. We keep them, too, because we're a well-run organization (also because we happen to be nice and charming and responsible).

Like any company, we have officers and rules

and record-keeping. I'm the chairman. I run the meetings and plan special events for our charges. I also try to think up new publicity ideas.

In case you can't tell, I'm kind of a loudmouth. (But lovable, too.) Here are some other things about me: I love sports and animals, and I *live* in casual clothes such as jeans and sweatshirts. Some of the others (Stacey, for instance) tease me about my lack of "fashion sense". I suppose I could have lots of chic outfits if I wanted them (my stepdad is pretty rich), but I can't be bothered. I'd probably just ruin them, anyway.

My stepdad, by the way, is called Watson Brewer. My mum married him a year or so ago. (My father walked out on our family when I was seven. It's something I don't like to talk about.) Watson must really love kids, because when he married her, he got me and my three brothers into the bargain. (Charlie's seventeen, Sam's fifteen, and David Michael's seven.) He has also got two kids from a previous marriage, Karen and Andrew, who live with him every other weekend. Then, to top it all off, Mum and Watson have adopted a little Vietnamese girl called Emily Michelle (who just happens to be the cutest child in the universe). Then my grandmother moved in to help out. Now *that's* a big family. Not that space is a problem. Our house is a huge old mansion right over on the other side of the town.

9

Kristy

It's so far from Claud's, Charlie has to drive me to and from BSC meetings.

I *used* to live across the street from the Kishis, before Mum remarried. I've known Claudia since we were both in nappies. Even then she liked sweets. I *still* can't work out how she stays so thin. Yes, Claudia the junk food fanatic has a figure like a model. She also has perfect skin. She's Japanese-American, with gorgeous black hair and almond-shaped eyes. And she can throw together the funkiest clothes and make them look good. That Friday, for instance, she was wearing ripped cut-off jeans held up by a frayed rope belt, a T-shirt with the collar torn off, huge white socks all bunched around the ankle, and old-fashioned black lace-up shoes. She looked totally cool.

Claud is our vice-chairman (mainly because we hold our meetings in her room). Her duties are answering the phone during non-meeting times and ruining our diets.

Although Claudia is one of my oldest friends, my *best* friend is Mary Anne Spier. People say we look a little alike (we're both short and we both have shoulder-length brown hair), but we're opposites in many ways. Mary Anne hates anything athletic. Also she's the shyest, most sensitive person I've ever met. She cries all the time. At films, *some* people cry at the sad parts. Mary Anne can tell when the sad parts are coming, and starts crying *in advance*.

10

To tell you the truth, I'd probably be sensitive, too, if my mum had died when I was a baby. Mary Anne was sent away to live with her grandparents until her dad recovered from the loss. Eventually Mr Spier took her back and brought her up by himself. He was extremely strict. Mary Anne had to dress in little-girl clothes and wear her hair in pigtails until the seventh grade. But that's all in the past now. Mr Spier has loosened up a lot (I'll tell you why later). Now Mary Anne definitely looks her age. *And* she happens to be the only member of the BSC who has a steady boyfriend! He's Logan Bruno, an associate member of the club, and he's cute and athletic and funny and all those good things. He also has this cool Southern accent.

Mary Anne is the BSC secretary. She handles our official record book—which includes our schedule of sitting jobs, an up-to-date client list, notes about our charges' special needs, and a record of fees that each client pays. Mary Anne also keeps track of our personal schedules (Jessi has regular ballet classes, Claudia takes art lessons, Mal goes to an orthodontist—stuff like that). She writes in this extra-neat handwriting, and she's never made a mistake. Talk about organized.

"Okay, it's official," Claudia announced. "Sample A wins four to three, with two un-decideds!" She turned over an index card that said SAMPLE A. The other side said SKOR.

11

Oh, by the way, all nine members were there, including our associate member. That's unusual for us, but Claud's room is big enough—just about.

"Hey, Skor scores!" Logan said.

"Congratulations," Stacey mumbled, chomping on some corn chips.

You may have noticed that two people didn't vote in the taste test. The "two abstentions" were for our health-food freaks, Stacey McGill and Dawn Schafer. Personally, I think health foods are for the birds (I mean that literally). Poor Stacey is *required* to stay away from sweets. She has diabetes, which means her body can't handle sugar. Because of that, she has to give herself (are you sitting down?) *injections* of something called insulin, every day.

Stacey is our treasurer. She collects weekly subs, which we use to help pay Claudia's phone bill, buy supplies, and contribute to my brother Charlie's petrol expenses. Stace is also our resident New Yawka (she doesn't talk like one, though). She moved here last year when her dad's company transferred him. Then she moved back to NYC when her dad's company transferred him back. Then she moved here *again*, but without her father. Yes, unfortunately, it was the big D. Divorce. Now she and her mum live in Stoneybrook in a small house (Stacey's an only child).

Stacey's really beautiful. And sophisticated (but *not* snobby). And clever (especially at

12

maths). Plus she is the BSC's other fashion expert. She doesn't look a thing like Claud, though. Stacey has long blonde hair and blue eyes. She also has a sleeker style of dressing. Shop-bought sensational, not thrown-together sensational like Claud. At our Friday meeting she was wearing this white T-shirt that hung practically to her knees (Stacey calls it a "jersey tunic" or something), white stretch pants ("ribbed leggings") to mid-calf, a tan leather belt over the T-shirt, and leather-strap sandals. Sometimes Stacey likes to wear all black, which seems kind of weird in the summer.

While we're on the subject of "weird", let me tell you about our other health-food person, Dawn Schafer. (*She's* not weird, just her taste in food.) Now, she doesn't have diabetes, so she *can* eat chocolate. But she just *doesn't*. She actually prefers health food. Stick a lump of tofu in front of her and she's happy. I have actually seen her turn down a steaming hot slice of pepperoni pizza for an avocado-and-salad sandwich on pitta bread. Honest.

Needless to say, Dawn is a real individualist. She stands up for what she calls her "alternate life-style". Maybe that's why she's our alternate officer. (Her job is to fill in whenever one of us is absent.)

Dawn has amazing hair. It's super-long, and so blonde it's almost white. She moved to

Stoneybrook last year from Southern California. She also comes from a divorced family. Her dad and her younger brother still live near Los Angeles. Her mum is a beautiful, absent-minded woman who does things like leaving car keys in the airing cupboard.

Now get this. Both Dawn's mum and Mary Anne's dad have remarried—to each other! That's right. It turned out that they were sweethearts ages ago at Stoneybrook High School. They started dating again when Dawn and her mum moved here. So now free-spirited Sharon Schafer and stodgy Richard Spier live under the same roof—and so do Mary Anne and Dawn, as stepsisters.

And *that's* one reason Mr Spier has loosened up. At least that's my theory.

Our junior officers, Jessi Ramsey and Mallory Pike, come from more typical families. (If there is such a thing as a typical family.) Well, I take that back. The Pikes have eight kids, including triplets. *Jessi* comes from a more typical family, with one younger brother and one younger sister.

Jessi and Mal are both eleven years old and in the sixth grade (the rest of us are thirteen-year-old eighth-graders). Their parents don't let them stay out late during the week, so they mostly take afternoon jobs. That works out well, because it frees the rest of us for later jobs. Jessi and Mal are great sitters—and best friends. Both of them

14

are into books, and they both complain that their parents treat them like babies. And they're both creative. Mal writes stories and illustrates them, and Jessi's an excellent ballerina (she takes lessons in Stamford, the nearest big city to Stoneybrook).

Physically they're nothing like each other. Jessi's black, and she has the long, long legs of a dancer. Mal is white, with red hair and ordinary legs. Mal also wears glasses and a brace (the clear kind).

That leaves our associate officers. I've already mentioned Logan, so I'll tell you a little about Shannon Kilbourne. She lives in my neighbourhood and goes to Stoneybrook Day School, a private school. She has lots of interests, so she belongs to a million after-school clubs. Recently at school, her music teacher had convinced Shannon that she could sing.

Which she had started doing in Claud's room, along with some hand gestures that I supposed were dance movements.

"Yoo-ee-yoo-ee-yoo-ee-yoo-ee," sang Shannon in a very soft voice.

At this point, my eyes were on Claud's digital clock. It read 5:29.

"Uh, Shannon," Claudia finally said. "Are you all right?"

Click. 5:30. "This meeting will come to order!" I announced.

15

Shannon stopped yoo-eeing.

"Any new business?" I asked.

No one answered for a moment. Then Claudia said, "I am dying to know what Shannon was doing."

Shannon smiled. "Just some vocal warm-ups. You know, for drama camp. Musical rehearsals start this week."

"Have they given you a part yet?" Jessi asked.

"Ado Annie in *Oklahoma*," Shannon replied.

"You are so lucky," Claudia said. "I mean, to be doing something *fun* this summer."

"You're all going to Sea City, right?" Shannon asked. "That's fun."

"Only Mal and Jessi and Stacey are going tomorrow," Claudia said. "The rest of us are going next week with Mrs Barrett's fiancé, Franklin. And *I* have to suffer five more days of summer school."

"Yuck," Shannon said.

"I still can't believe I'm so stupid at maths that I had to go. I mean, if you do badly in art class, or music, they don't make you go to summer school." Claudia sighed. "I'm depressed. Time for some Rolos."

She jumped off her bed and plunged into the wardrobe. When she came out, she was holding a shoebox full of packets of Rolos, Kit-Kats and Maltesers.

As we grabbed and ripped wrappers and munched, the phone rang.

Claudia swallowed quickly and picked up the receiver. "Hello, Babysitters Club. . . . Oh, hi, Myriah! You want to talk to her? Okay." She held the phone out to Mary Anne.

"Hi, Myriah," said Mary Anne. "The last day is Friday. . . . No, it'll be over in time. Don't worry, I've worked it out with Kristy. You can play. Okay, 'bye."

When she hung up, she turned to me and said, "Myriah was worried that Mini-Camp would clash with the Krushers game."

"She's always worried about that," I replied. "It shows she's interested."

"You should have seen her yesterday at Mini-Camp," Mary Anne said. "She drew this box on the side of the barn and spent half the day trying to throw a ball inside the lines."

"The strike zone," I informed her. (See what I mean about Mary Anne and sports?)

"Uh-huh," Mary Anne replied. "Only she brought Chewy that day and he kept chasing after the ball." (Chewy is short for Chewbacca, the Perkinses' Labrador retriever.)

Dawn laughed. "Then we had 'art corner', and Chewy decided to whack his tail into the paint bottles."

"We got the paint off the patio," Mary Anne added. "But the grass looks sort of tie-dyed."

17

"It's been fun, though," Dawn said. "I'll be so sad to see Mini-Camp end."

Mary Anne sighed. "Yeah . . ."

I knew the waterworks were about to start. So I piped up, "Well, the Krushers are looking good. Only a week till our big showdown."

Our final opponents were going to be Bart's Bashers. As usual. (They're practically the only team we play.)

The Krushers and the Bashers are sort-of homemade teams. I organized the Krushers with kids who were too young or too afraid to play Little League or T-Ball. I'm not sure why Bart Taylor organized his team. (Bart is a very important topic. Much more on him later.)

"Too bad we're going to miss it," Mal said.

"Yeah, it'll be really tough lying on the beach all day," I replied.

"Soaking up rays," Dawn said.

"Swimming," Claudia chimed in.

"Meeting cute lifeguards," Shannon added.

Mallory giggled. "Oooh, I can't *wait*!"

"Me neither!" Jessi squealed. "I am sooo excited. Your parents were so nice to let me come. I'm going to be the best mother's helper ever."

Stacey sighed. "You know, I sort of wish I were going to the Pikes' instead of the Barretts'. I'll feel so strange being down there in a different house."

"Don't worry, Stace," Mary Anne said.

"You'll be fine. Besides, you'll be next door to us. All the kids'll be playing together."

"I wonder if I'll run into you-know-who," Stacey said.

Mary Anne looked down and cleared her throat. "You will."

"That guy's going to be down there? The one who dumped Stacey?" I blurted out. (Tactful as ever.)

"Yeah," Mary Anne said. "I got a letter from Alex. Toby's got a job as a mother's helper."

Stacey rolled her eyes. "Oh, groan. The last person I want to see."

I glanced at Logan. He did *not* look happy when Mary Anne mentioned Alex. The last time Mary Anne was in Sea City, she and Alex had become pretty friendly. Nothing serious, just a couple of casual dates. Mary Anne is the loyal type—and Logan is *not* the jealous type. Still, I could tell Alex wasn't Logan's favourite topic.

The room had fallen silent. I thought fast. I knew Logan was working part-time at the Rosebud Cafe this summer, and that the Pikes had invited him to Sea City the next weekend. So I said, "I bet you'll be happy to get away from your job for a couple of days."

Logan's tense expression melted away. "Yeah," he said, smiling at Mary Anne. "I can't wait."

2nd CHAPTER

Claudia

Friday

Dear Stacey,

By the time this card arrives, you will be at Sea City! Yea! I am sooooo jellous! But I miss you! Except I'm going to see you in about an hour at the meting.... ?????? But when you read this, I will be missing you.

Are you having a good time? I hop so. Me, I am counting the days til sumer school is over! I can do that now — count. See what a anducational experiense its been?

Mabe when I com down we can have a bon fire. Then I will finly have a perfict use for my maths notebook!

Love, Claudia

Claudia

It was torture.

Going to summer school, I mean. Let's face it, it's bad enough just to *have* to go. For me it was especially embarrassing, because of my sister. Her name is Janine. I call her Janine the Genius. And she is one. Her I.Q. is high enough for two people. She can solve maths problems in her sleep. Janine was going to summer classes, too—but they were at Stoneybrook University, and she was taking them because she *wanted* to. (My parents, of course, think Janine can do no wrong.)

Then there's summer school itself. They cram all the grades into one place, the high school. Half the kids are these huge sixteen-and seventeen-year-olds who don't want to be there—and look much bigger and angrier than you. And the other half are little kids who don't want to be there either—and walk around with these pathetic, scared faces.

I thought a long time about it. Now I have this theory. The Claudia Kishi Theory of Summer School Torture. You see, the teachers like to take summers off, too. So the worst thing in the world is to have stupid kids at school. The kids have to make up classes, which means some teachers have to *teach* the classes.

If *you* were a teacher who had to give up your holiday for summer school, how would you feel? I know I'd be furious.

21

So that's why they make summer school the most miserable place in the world: REVENGE!

I suppose they think they'll scare you into getting good grades the next year. They make it so horrible you'll never want to come back. Like prison.

Who knows, next summer they may have a rock pile.

I did end up working *hard*. I even understood the stuff.

Anyway, my class lasted for a month. The first week I felt as if I were in another town. I knew *nobody*. Everyone looked so glum and unfriendly.

The second week I got to know some of the kids. And you know what? Most of them were pretty cool.

On Monday of that week, a crowd of us stopped at the ice cream van on the way home. "Now let's see," said this girl named Theresa, as we walked with our pops. "If the guy has twenty-two ice cream bars that cost him fifty cents each, sells one to each of us for a dollar fifty, then . . . how much did his toupee cost?"

I nearly spat out my ice cream. "Stop!"

"Can we use a calculator?" asked Carly, another classmate.

We laughed all the way home. The more we joked about how stupid we were, the closer we felt.

It turned out Carly lives near me. Over the

22

week we became pretty good friends. She's a fantastic watercolourist and potter. She even has a potter's wheel in her basement.

You know what the best thing was? Eventually the kids in my class started calling me "the brainy one". *Me*. Claudia, the Blot on the Kishi Family Tree.

So the good news was that despite the Torture Theory, and despite the fact that I *hated* the work, summer school actually wasn't so bad.

By the Friday of the BSC meeting, I was having mixed feelings. I was glad school was almost over, but I wondered what would happen to my new friendships. What if Carly and Theresa and I weren't in the same classes in the autumn? Most of us were starting to feel pretty sad—especially Carly. I could sense she knew how strong my BSC friendships were.

I tried not to think of the future. And I vowed I'd write to Carly when I was on my *real* holiday.

It was hard to stay in a good mood at the BSC meeting. There was Shannon, on the way to stardom at summer camp. Jessi, Mal, and Stacey were a day away from fun and sun. Mary Anne and Dawn were all starry-eyed about Mini-Camp. And Kristy was her usual gung-ho self about the Krushers.

Thank goodness I was going to Sea City. I kept thinking about that. Every time I imagined Jessi or Stacey or Mal on the beach, I'd just imagine myself there with them.

Only eight days and counting! I could practically feel the ocean breeze.

But first I'd have to say goodbye to the others. When Saturday came, Kristy, Mary Anne, Dawn, and I met at the Pikes' house.

Do you know what it's like when a family of ten is leaving to go on holiday? It gives *chaos* new meaning. It's like cattle-rustling in an old Western.

Except cattle are much quieter than the Pike kids.

Jessi had slept over the night before. As I walked up the Pikes' lawn, she struggled out of the house with two suitcases.

She smiled and said, "Hi, Clau—"

Claire charged out of the house. "Where's Thomas?"

"Who's Thomas?" Jessi asked.

"My new stuffed bear," Claire whined. "I can't find him!"

"Did you pack him?"

"I don't know."

"Let's check." Jessi put the suitcases down on the front step and opened one.

At that moment Margo's voice screamed from inside, "*Stop*, Nicky!"

24

I could hear her footsteps go *tap-tap-tap-tap-tap-tap*—

"Watch it!" Jessi cried.

Margo had run out of the front door. The *taps* stopped when her foot landed inside Claire's open suitcase.

"No!" shouted Claire.

"Whoa!" shouted Margo.

Margo went flying onto the lawn. Claire's suitcase followed her, spilling clothes and toys and books. Jessi ran to Margo. I rushed over to help. Nicky appeared in the doorway, his mouth hanging open.

"Are you okay?" Jessi and I asked Margo at the same time.

"Did Nicky touch me?" was her reply.

"I *didn't*," Nicky said.

Margo burst into tears. "He was trying to lick me and give me his nit germs!"

Jessi and I looked at each other, then at Nicky. By now, most of the other kids—and Mr Pike—had come to the door.

"Nicholas," Mr Pike said very seriously. "Please come into the living room. We need to have a talk."

"Oooh, Nicky," teased Adam. Or Byron. Or Jordan. (I wasn't really looking at them, so it was hard to tell. They're identical triplets.)

As Nicky slunk inside, Claire cried, "Here he

25

is!" She held up a grey stuffed bear with a scarf around its neck.

"Thomas?" Jessi asked.

With a huge smile, Claire hugged the bear. "Thomas-silly-billy-goo-goo!"

She turned and began to skip into the house.

"Uh, Claire," Jessi said. "Would you help me pick up all this stuff?"

"*Margo* knocked it over," Claire replied.

"*Jessi* was the one who opened it on the step," Margo shot back.

For a moment—just a teeny moment—I was *glad* I was going to summer school instead of to Sea City.

Mal bustled out of the front door with a couple more suitcases. "Uh-oh," she said. "Let's see if we can pack Claire's suitcase in world record time!"

Well, that seemed to do the trick. Everyone pitched in and stuffed the suitcase again.

Then the kids ran back into the house, screaming with excitement. Mal and Jessi and I carried the suitcases to the cars.

"Hi!" Dawn called from down the street. She and Mary Anne were walking towards the house.

"Hi!" Jessi, Mal, and I called back.

Mary Anne pointed to a minivan in the Pikes' drive. "Whose is that?"

"My mum and dad rented it," Mal replied.

26

Dawn looked puzzled. "But you've got two estate cars."

"Well, we're bringing twelve people to Sea City," Mal said, pulling open the rear of the van. "And since you lot and Logan are all arriving next week with Franklin and his kids, and *they're* leaving with only Logan on Monday, that means we'll be coming home with . . . um . . ."

We counted in our heads. "Sixteen!" I announced. (Summer school had done me good.)

"Right," Mal said. "So Dad thought we would be more comfortable with a van and an estate car."

Honk! Honk!

The Junk Bucket was turning into the drive. That's the name of Charlie Thomas's car. Kristy was practically hanging out of the window, waving.

Honestly, that car is so old and rusty and clankety, I don't know why it doesn't fall apart. (Kristy's rich neighbours must *love* it.)

" 'Bye!" Kristy yelled.

"We're not going yet!" Jessi reassured her.

When Kristy got out, Charlie tooted the horn a couple of times and headed back home.

The Pikes' door opened again, and the rest of the family came tramping out. They were carrying suitcases, rucksacks, fishing gear, flippers, water wings, life jackets, you name it.

"I'm going in the van!" Adam yelled.

27

"Me too!" cried Nicky.

"Me too!" the rest of the kids screamed.

"I said it first!"

"*I* did!"

Mr Pike let out a whistle. In a loud voice, he announced who was going in which vehicle. Of course, this was followed by a chorus of "Not fair!" and "Can we swap on the way back?" and "I'm hungry!"

Soon everyone was handing us stuff to pack into the car and van. Mr and Mrs Pike knew exactly how to stack everything to make it all fit.

Vanessa Pike stood next to us with an excited smile. That usually means she is about to recite a poem (Vanessa loves to speak in rhyme). "As we pack up for New Jersey," she said, "everything is topsy-turvy."

In the back seat of the estate car, Nicky groaned loudly. "That doesn't rhyme, mushbrain!" he cried.

Vanessa put her hands on her hips. "Sticks and stones may break my bones—"

"And we all hate your stupid poems!" Adam bellowed from the van.

"*That* doesn't rhyme, either!" Vanessa retorted.

"If there is any more arguing, we are *not* stopping for ice cream," Mrs Pike said. "Now come on!"

Before long, we had finished packing and the

kids were in the car. Then Stacey came jogging over from the Pikes' back garden. (She and her mum live in the house behind the Pikes'.) "Hi, everyone," she said. "I came to say goodbye. The Barretts are going to pick me up in a few minutes."

On her face was this half-happy, half-sad expression. I could see Mary Anne's lips start to quiver. "Oh . . ." she said. "I'll miss you!"

"Me too!" Stacey replied. She and Mary Anne hugged and rocked back and forth.

Then Mal and Jessi and I said, "Ohhhhh," and went into a three-way hug.

"Hey, we're only going to be separated for a week," said Kristy, the Voice of Sanity.

We agreed that Kristy was right. Eventually Jessi hopped into the estate car and Mal climbed into the van.

" 'Bye!" the rest of us called out as the caravan began moving. "See you soon!"

" 'Bye!" answered Jessi and a couple of the other kids (the rest were grabbing and fidgeting and getting tangled in seat belts).

"Tell Mrs Barrett we'll meet her at the petrol station!" Mrs Pike called out.

"Okay!" I replied. We waved until they'd disappeared. Then we ran through the Pikes' garden to Stacey's house. Mrs McGill was smiling, but looked a little worried. "Now, you have packed your injection kit?" she asked.

29

"Yes, Mum," Stacey said patiently.

"And you have the number for the doctor down there, just in case?"

"Yes, Mum."

"We're hee-ere!" Buddy Barrett's voice shouted from the drive.

Stacey looked at Mary Anne, Kristy, Dawn, and me. "Ohhh . . ."

We all hugged *again*. Mary Anne started bawling. To tell you the truth, I was a bit misty-eyed myself (but maybe it was because I was thinking of summer school).

We followed Stacey to the front garden. She grabbed her suitcase, which was on the porch, and ran to the car. Mrs Barrett helped her jam it into the boot. We mentioned the petrol station to Mrs Barrett. She thanked us, climbed into the driver's seat, and pulled away.

The car jumped the kerb, then drove onto the road.

" 'Byyyyeeee!" the cry rang out along Elm Street.

Sigh.

Some of us were on our way.

I felt pretty good, though. Because it meant *my* trip was that much closer!

3rd CHAPTER

Mallory

Saturday

Hi, Dawn!

Well, we're here! What a trip. Everybody was so noisy. When we stopped for lunch, Nicky insisted on getting a large chocolate milkshake with extra ice cream. But only because the triplets each got one. Well, guess who barfed all over the rented van later on? It was gross. Dad had to drive to a car wash where they had a water hose and a wet vacuum. So the rest of the way the carpet was squishy and the van smelled. Everybody wanted to ride in the estate car after that. Poor Nicky. (Poor us, too.)

Jessi says hi! More on the Pike saga tomorrow.

Miss ya,
Love, Mal

"One!" Vanessa squealed.

We were about an hour away from Stoney-brook. Vanessa, Nicky, and Claire had decided to play some sort of secret game. For a long time they'd been staring out of the window. Now they were collapsing into giggles in their seats.

I hadn't been paying much attention to them. I was too busy reading my book, *The Golden Key* by George MacDonald, which was taking a lot of concentration.

"One what?" I said, looking up.

They all giggled again. I went back to my book.

About ten minutes later, Nicky blurted out, "Two!"

More hysterical giggles.

I happened to be looking out of the window when they got to "Four." That was when I realized what they were doing—counting people in other cars who were picking their noses.

So mature.

"Come on, let's play a new game," I suggested. "I'll start a story and everybody will add to it."

"Nooo," Nicky complained.

"Okay, you don't have to play, Nicky," I said. "Vanessa: Once upon a time there was a big fat toad who ate something very strange. Your turn."

"Um . . . It was a bogey from an old man with a bushy moustache!" she said, convulsing with laughter again.

32

"Then he turned green and sprouted hair from his ears!" Nicky added, suddenly interested.

"And went to the barber to have his ears cut off," Claire said.

We continued this until everyone was laughing too hard to go on.

Before long Vanessa asked, "When are we going to stop?"

"When we get past New York City," Dad said. "I agreed with Mum and Mrs Barrett to stop at the Little Chef, like we always do."

"If you had a car phone you could phone them and tell them to stop now!" Nicky said, pouting.

"Which is why I don't have a car phone," Dad mumbled.

"What?" Nicky said.

"Oh, nothing," Dad replied. I smiled at him.

Well, getting past New York ended up taking a lifetime. We got stuck in traffic between two enormous lorries for about half an hour.

By the time we reached the Little Chef, we were *starving*.

I suppose that's why Nicky thought he could drink that humongous milkshake. I don't need to go into the gory details—except to say that the Pike Family Barf Bucket was in the *wrong* car for this trip.

I sat by the window after that. It seemed a good place to be after Nicky's little accident. But I'd forgotten about New Jersey's fragrant industrial area. It's miles and miles of huge metal tanks surrounded by spiral stairs and blinking lights. It looks like a convention of spaceships. And it smells like a sewer.

It was hard to say which was better, inside or out.

Vanessa made the most of the situation. She had new material for her poetry. "Mister Smee and Captain Hook, ran away from Nicky's puke!"

"Vanessa!" Dad said warningly from the front seat.

I gave her a Look. Nicky was curled up in his seat, trying to sleep it off. I went back to my book.

"Hurry up and get a scarf! Please wipe up this pile of—"

"*Vanessa!*" This time Dad and I yelled at the same time.

"Sto-o-o-p," Nicky moaned.

I thought the trip would never end. My eyes were just closing when Dad said, "Uh-oh, do you see what I see?"

I sat up. We were zooming past a familiar sign. "'Sea City, Exit Ten Miles,'" I read aloud.

Claire started squealing. Vanessa screamed out, "Sea City, here we come!" Even Nicky came to life.

As we approached the Jersey coast, the scenery changed drastically. All these memories from past trips came back. The air became at least ten degrees cooler. I could smell the ocean. The soil

34

along the road was sandy and the trees were scrubby. Seagulls screeched overhead.

The kids were jumping with excitement when Dad drove off the exit ramp. We travelled for a few minutes more and came to a huge, reedy marsh. Across the marsh was a loooong, narrow road, built up on a jetty of rocks all cemented together.

We knew that road well. It is the only way to get to Sea City.

"The bridge! The bridge!" Claire piped up.

"It's not a bridge," Vanessa corrected her. "It's a causeway. Here we go driving to the beach—"

"Hey, Vanessa," Nicky interrupted. "What rhymes with causeway?"

The van was silent for the next few minutes. I closed my eyes and breathed in the salty air.

Just over the causeway, a three-dimensional purple cow loomed over the road on a billboard. That's our first important landmark on the way to Sea City. "The cow!" Claire shouted.

I pointed to our second landmark, a roadside restaurant. "Crabs for Grabs!"

But the third landmark had changed. It used to be a billboard for suntan lotion, which showed a dog pulling down a little girl's bathing suit. Now it was an add for a new local hot dog place.

"Looooook," Nicky said sadly, as if he'd just

been told Sea City had washed away forever. "The rude picture's gone."

"What does the sign say?" Claire asked.

"'Weiner's Wieners,'" I read.

Well, that was good enough. The little girl's bare bottom was instantly forgotten in a fit of giggling.

Sea City is on a curved piece of land (a "spit" of land, Dad calls it) that juts into the ocean like a long tail. It seems like an island, but technically it's not. There are patches of marsh connecting it to the "mainland."

Once it *turned* into an island, though. According to the Sea City guidebook, a huge storm washed out the marsh and the causeway. But that was ages ago.

We zoomed onto Sea City's main road. Suddenly we were surrounded. Hot dog stands, souvenir shops, seafood restaurants, fish markets. The crackling sound of frying food everywhere. "There's Trampoline Land!" Nicky shouted.

"And miniature golf!" Vanessa said.

In the distance I could see the huge Ferris wheel arching over the boardwalk. And I could hear crashing sounds that could only be one thing—the ocean.

We had arrived. I couldn't wait to see our house.

A stiff breeze was blowing as we pulled into our

drive. I could tell because the wind chimes on the front porch were tinkling, and the white wicker swing was rocking back and forth.

I love our Sea City house. We rent the same one every year. It's Victorian-style, a big gingerbread cottage with yellow and white trim. There are gables and eaves and posts everywhere. And three whole floors.

You know what the best part is? It *faces* the ocean.

"Oooooh, honeysuckle, honeysuckle!" Vanessa cried, running to the blossoming bush.

"Makes me want to laugh and chuckle!" Nicky said. "Hey, Vanessa, did you hear that?"

Nicky was very proud of himself, but Vanessa was too busy sniffing away to pay attention.

The estate car pulled up just moments later. "Let's go to the beach!" Adam and Margo were screaming.

"Let's unpack!" Mum answered.

I have to admit, it was hard to unload the car when the beach was staring us in the face. But this year I was not only the oldest Pike kid, I was a mother's helper (*parents'* helper would be more accurate).

Somehow Dad, Mum, Jessi, and I managed to help everybody settle in. Jessi and I bagged the yellow-wallpapered bedroom on the first floor, where Mary Anne and Stacey stayed when they had been parents' helpers last time.

"I *love* this view!" Jessi said, gazing out of the window. Her grin was so big, I thought her face would crack. "I can't believe how beautiful Sea City is!"

"Hi, up there!"

We looked down to see Stacey with Buddy and Suzi Barrett (Buddy's seven and Suzi's five). "Hi!" we both called.

"We're going to claim the beach!" Buddy said.

"Us too!" cried some voices from below and above us. Instantly the Pike herd began stampeding. Their footsteps rattled the stairs.

"We'd better go," I said to Jessi.

In a few moments we found ourselves running through the sand towards the ocean.

I have never seen Jessi so happy. She was like a little kid, jumping and screaming.

Stacey had run ahead of us. She was already talking to two boys, near a couple of blankets close to the beach. A group of kids was busy digging sand castles nearby. Our charges quickly joined them.

Typical Stacey, I thought. She *would* find the boys right away. Once she had this huge crush on a lifeguard called Scott, who unfortunately had no interest in her. Then she met a boy named Toby. He was the cousin of a parents' helper named Alex. Alex and Mary Anne became good friends, and Stacey and Toby actually went out together. But poor Stacey had bad luck again. He broke up with her at the end of the holiday.

I stopped in my tracks when I saw the guy's face. He *was* Toby. I remembered him. The same wavy brown hair, freckles, deep brown eyes . . .

Deep, *luscious* brown eyes. Wow, he was cute. I didn't remember *that* about him.

"So, you're going to be here a while?" I heard him say to Stacey.

"Mm-hm," Stacey replied.

"Perfect tanning day," Toby said. "Huh?"

Stacey shrugged. "I suppose so." Then she looked away and shouted, "Suzi, stay away from the water!"

"Who's bringing Mary Anne down?" asked the other boy.

I tore my eyes away from Toby for a moment. The other guy was fairer-skinned and had lighter brown hair. It took me a minute to realize he was Alex.

"The boyfriend of the woman I'm working for," Stacey said. "Uh, excuse me." She went running off towards Suzi, who really wasn't doing anything unsafe, as far as *I* could see.

"Oh, hi," Toby said, looking at me. "I'm Toby and this is my cousin Alex. I don't think we've met."

"Mal," I said. "I mean, I'm Mallory Pike." My voice sounded as if I'd swallowed a fur ball.

39

Toby's eyes widened. "*Pike?* Are you one of the ones Stacey and Mary Anne used to sit for?"

I felt deflated. "Yeah. But now I'm sitting, too."

Toby seemed to find that funny. "I can believe that. You certainly have changed."

"Well, it happens," I said, laughing.

"Yeah."

Soon we separated to watch our charges. But I could see Toby looking at me off and on during the afternoon. And smiling, too.

Could it be? It didn't seem possible. He was so much *older*. Fifteen, probably.

But I liked the way he was making me feel. I'd never felt that way before.

4th CHAPTER

Stacey

saturday

Dear Claud,

   Sea City is beautiful. The weather is great. The kids are having a fantastic time.

   Buddy wasn't too bad on the trip down. Did you know Mrs Barrett is a nervous driver? Well, she is. Being in heavy traffic with her was NOT fun. The trip seemed REALLY long.

   I don't know why, but today was harder work than I expected. Maybe it's just me. I saw <u>Toby</u> today (gag me!) and I think that got things off to a weird start.

   Oh, well. I'm happy to be here. Really. And I can't wait for you to come.

Love,
Stacey 41

Let me say it straight out. I *hated* my first day at Sea City.

I don't know why I was being so polite in my card to Claudia. Maybe I thought someone at the Sea City post office would read it and tell Mrs Barrett.

What I really wanted to say was this: Mrs Barrett was being a big pain in the neck.

Usually I like her. For one thing, she is stunning. She seems younger than a lot of mums. She wears the coolest clothes, which look great on her incredible, Cosmo-model figure. Her hair is a gorgeous chestnut colour, with natural curls that spill to her shoulders. I would *love* to look like her when I'm older.

Her personality? Well, nice but disorganized. She's famous for calling the BSC during non-meeting times. Which isn't all her fault. She's divorced and has to take care of three kids on her own. Buddy's the oldest, and he's a handful. He's a skinny eight-year-old who can't seem to sit still. His sister Suzi, who's five, is a cute little pudge who loves to play pretend. And Marnie's an adorable two-year-old with curly blonde hair and blue eyes.

I was looking forward to being her helper—and going to Sea City. But I felt a little funny not working for the Pikes. Twice before I'd gone to the beach with them, and I loved it.

I understood, though, that Mal was old enough

now to be responsible, and Jessi's her best friend. And the Barretts' house was next door to the Pikes', so it wasn't as if I wouldn't see them.

Anyway, by the time we left Stoneybrook, I was totally psyched. Mrs Barrett was excited and friendly when she picked me up. She kept thanking me for coming.

I should have known I was in for trouble when she drove onto the kerb, just outside her house.

"Oh!" she cried. "What did I do?"

"My dad does that all the time," I said as the car bumped back onto the street. "He grew up in New York City, so he didn't get his licence till he was in his twenties."

That little story is usually interesting to grown-ups. But Mrs Barrett simply said "Mm-hm," and clutched the steering wheel tighter.

Just outside Stoneybrook, Buddy began asking, "When are we going to stop?"

"Buddy, can't you see I'm driving?" Mrs Barrett snapped. "I have to follow the Pikes or we'll get lost."

I was sitting in the front. I turned round to face the kids. Marnie was already drifting off to sleep in her car seat. "Come on, Buddy and Suzi," I said. "Let's see who can spot the most out-of-state licence plates."

I explained the game to Suzi. They played for a pretty long time, but Mrs Barrett's mood didn't improve.

Honnnnnnk! "Stay in your lane, you creep!" she yelled to someone who pulled in between her and the Pikes.

Scrreeeeek! She slammed on the brakes when someone swerved towards her from an entrance ramp. The car skidded a little, and she screamed.

Suzi shrieked. Buddy looked pale with shock. Marnie woke up crying. Mrs Barrett said—well, I won't say what she said.

Things just went from bad to worse. We got stuck in a traffic jam on the motorway by New York City. *And* we lost sight of both Pike cars.

I reminded Mrs Barrett that we'd agreed to meet the Pikes at a Little Chef in New Jersey. That made her feel a *little* better.

We did all catch up at the Little Chef. But Marnie decided she wanted to live there. She absolutely, positively did not want to spend another minute in the car.

The problem was, we had a good hour to go.

And she didn't stop crying for even a second.

Then the Pikes had to get off the motorway when Nicky was sick. Well, Mrs Barrett got hysterical trying to work out what was wrong. She was convinced we were lost.

By the time we reached the Sea City causeway, Mrs Barrett's knuckles were white around the steering wheel.

"I've got to go to the toilet!" Buddy cried.

"I want apple juice!" Suzi whined.

"*Waaaaaaaaah!*" Marnie shrieked.

I was a wreck. Even the purple cow didn't make me smile.

Next to the Pikes' house, the Barretts' looked tiny. And not nearly as old. It was a plain, white-shingled bungalow with chrysanthemums and rhododendrons growing in front. It looked as though it had been built on what had been the side garden of the Pikes' house.

But when we stopped inside, Mrs Barrett became human again.

"Stacey, thanks for being so patient with me," she said as we were unpacking the suitcases (the kids were busy changing into their swimsuits). "This is just such a new experience for me. It's my first holiday as a single parent. It's the longest I've ever driven. It's the first time I've hired a mother's helper." She let out a deep breath, then smiled warmly. "I—I just feel a little over-whelmed, you know?"

I smiled back. "That's okay. Why don't I take the kids to the beach and give you a chance to rest?"

Her face brightened. "Thanks. Just don't forget the sun tan lotion."

I felt much better. I gathered the kids and slathered them with lotion (the old gather and slather). Then we ran to the Pikes'.

In minutes we were storming the beach

45

together. The wind and sun felt *wonderful*. The sand tickled my feet. A wave broke on the shore, and I could feel its cool mist. My last bit of tension just melted away.

And that was when I saw Toby.

He tried to be so friendly. How could he even *face* me after dumping me? What nerve!

I was determined not to let him ruin my trip. I hardly said a word to him. I pretended the kids needed me and I ran away.

Toby's and my charges played together at first, then drifted apart. That was fine with me. I didn't look at him, didn't even *think* of him again.

Until suppertime.

As the kids ran back into the houses, screaming and laughing, Mal pulled me aside. "Uh, Stacey . . . are you and Toby, like, you know, still . . .?"

"Mal," I said, "if a great white shark were to hop up on the beach and drag him away, I wouldn't mind a bit."

Mal's eyes opened wide. "Really?"

"Well, I might feel sorry for the shark," I said. "Why?"

Mal giggled. "Well, um, it's just that . . . I think he likes me."

"*Whaaaat*?" I didn't mean to sound so surprised. I didn't mean to imply that Mallory wasn't attractive to boys. But I hadn't expected to hear her say that.

"He was so sweet to me, Stacey," she said.

46

"And the way he was looking at me . . . I could just
tell—"

I exhaled. "Mal, don't get your hopes up."

"What do you mean?" She looked crushed.

"Look, it's not that he *wouldn't* be interested in
you. It's just . . . it's just *him*, that's all. He's a
smooth talker, Mallory. He seems so cool and
friendly. But if you ever got involved with him,
you'd just get hurt. He'd dump you like he
dumped me."

Mal's brow was furrowed. "Well, how do you
know? I mean, maybe he's changed—"

I was losing my patience. The idea that that
dweeb would flirt with an eleven-year-old made
me furious. "Take my advice, Mal. Forget Toby.
That's all I want to say. I have to help Mrs Barrett
with dinner."

I began to walk towards the house. I heard
Mal say, "I think you're . . . you're *jealous*,
Stacey."

"What?" I said.

"If you don't like him any more, then you
shouldn't mind if he likes *me*," Mal went on.
"Besides, just because I'm younger than you
doesn't mean I'm a *baby*. I can take care of myself
with boys!"

With that, she marched into her house.

Mallory and Toby? This was the last thing I
needed.

5th CHAPTER

Dawn

Monday

Dear Jessi,
I think "Club Mad" might have been a good name for Mini-Camp, after all.

Today was going to be a fun, simple day. Collages, snack, and a visit to the Stones' farm. We had planned it so carefully.

It was a disaster. Worse than that, a fiasco (I think that's worse). Well, whatever. Now, when you walk in our garden, your footsteps crunch. And poor Mrs Stone is going to have to send her animals

48

to a psychiatrist. I'd go into the details, but it'll be more fun to tell you in person.

FIVE MORE DAYS!!!!!!!!!

Oh, some good news. I called Franklin to ask about our ride, and he wants me to sit for his kids next weekend.

That's all for now. Mary Anne says hi.

Luv, Dawn

Hi!

"Which ones are hard-boiled?" I shouted, gazing into our fridge. I saw three egg cartons, neatly stacked on the bottom shelf.

"The two cartons on the right," Mary Anne called from the garden. She was busily setting up for the midday arrival of our Mini-Campers.

"But all three cartons are in one pile!" I replied.

"Oh, Dad must have restacked them," Mary Anne said. "Just take an egg from each and spin it."

"Huh?"

"Bring them all outside. I'll do it."

I picked up the cartons and walked out of the back door. Mary Anne had placed our picnic table

49

and a card table next to each other, side by side. On them was a stack of coloured paper; three bottles of glue; containers filled with small sea-shells, sand, and uncooked macaroni; and some smaller empty containers. (We had got permission to take the sand from a neighbourhood playground, and Mary Anne had collected the shells in Sea City.)

Today's first project was my idea, "Summer Collages". I decided it would be a great way to start our last week of Mini-Camp—impressions of the summer gone by and adventures yet to come.

Mini-Camp had been hard work, but a lot of fun. We'd done face-painting and "sand sculpture" (layers of coloured sand in a small bottle), and taken a trip to the Stoneybrook Fire Department. We'd even had a dramatic presentation of the Dr Seuss book, *The Lorax*. (I think environmental issues are really important. If you don't know what *The Lorax* has to do with that, you should read the book.)

"What's this about spinning the egg?" I asked Mary Anne as I put the cartons on the picnic table.

"Watch." She took one from the top carton and spun it on its side. "That's hard-boiled." Then she took an egg from the carton underneath and spun *that* one. It turned only once or twice, *very* wobbly. "That's raw. It does that because of the liquid inside."

50

Dawn

I smiled. "You're a genius."

Mary Anne actually blushed. I carefully replaced the raw egg. Before I could take the carton inside, I heard a voice scream out, "Hiiii!"

We turned to see Jenny "Our Angel" Prezzioso running towards us. She's a four-year-old who lives next door, and she's one of our campers. ("Our Angel" is what her parents call her, but she *isn't*. She's pretty spoiled.)

"Hi!" Mary Anne and I both called back.

"What are we doing today?" Jenny asked.

I put the carton down and began to explain the project. Soon the other kids started filtering in: first Myriah Perkins, who's five; Jamie Newton (four); Charlotte Johanssen (eight); and Mathew and Johnny Hobart (six and four).

"Okay," Mary Anne announced, "today we're making summer collages. We have things here you can use. But first you have to find your own materials. Take the empty containers and go and collect some natural objects that you can glue to your papers."

"Things that remind you of summer and Mini-Camp," I added.

The kids grabbed the containers and took off. Charlotte came back first, with grass clippings, leaves, a dandelion, and some twigs. She got to work with the glue.

Before long all the kids were at their places, gluing away. Mary Anne sat beside them,

51

breaking some hard-boiled eggs. She put the inside parts into one container (to be used for egg salad later) and the shells into another. "You can use the sand, macaroni, and eggshells for different textures," she said.

Mathew Hobart was holding two small seashells over his eyes. Before I could work out what he was doing, he'd managed to hold them in place by lowering his eyebrows over them. "Hi!" he said, turning blindly to his left and right.

Well, everyone hooted with laughter. The kids tried to copy him. "Come on, everyone," Mary Anne said, "some of those edges are—"

"Owwwwww!" Jamie Newton cried. A tiny trail of blood began to trickle from a cut high on his right cheek.

"Ooh, let me clean that up," Mary Anne said.

As they walked inside, I heard a *splat* behind me.

I turned to see Myriah Perkins staring at her collage. A broken raw egg was spreading across it. "Ooops," she said. "I thought they were hard-boiled."

Well, we all shrieked about *that*. Myriah had taken the liberty of reaching into the nearest egg carton (left there by yours truly).

The kids were getting silly now. Johnny began pouring glue on top of the egg.

"Ugh!" Marilyn, Myriah, and Jenny yelled.

"Johnny, no!" I said.

52

Crunch. Jenny had sat on . . . something. She'd stopped laughing. Slowly she stood up and looked underneath her.

Another egg was there. This one was hard-boiled. And squashed into a white-and-yellow mishmash.

Mathew was laughing so hard he fell over.

"Mathew Hobart," I scolded, "did you do that?"

"I'm going to tell!" Jenny said. "My bottom's going to be all *yucky*!"

The kids were really getting carried away. Even Charlotte was laughing, and she's the most mature, serious kid I know.

I could see it was time to move on. I helped wipe off the back of Jenny's shorts. As soon as Mary Anne returned, I said, "Uh, I think we should go to the Stones'."

Jamie seemed to be fine. He even looked proud of the little plaster on his cheek. Mary Anne said, "I'll call Mrs Stone to make sure it's okay to come early."

Johnny was now pretending a clump of grass was a moustache. Myriah was trying to make macaroni into fangs. Charlotte, of course, was making a beautiful collage.

"She says it's okay!" Mary Anne said, running out of the house. "Let's go and see the animals!"

"Yeaaa!"

We left for our Mini-Camp Day at the Farm.

(This was Mary Anne's idea, and a great one.)
Down the road from us is a real little farm, owned
by this friendly couple, Mr and Mrs Stone. They
have the cutest baby goat called Elvira, and guess
what? Mary Anne and I actually goat-sat Elvira
for a few days when the Stones were away for a
while.

It's a loooong walk, all the way past the
cemetery on the outskirts of town. But the kids
were so excited they didn't mind. They began
running when they heard Mrs Stone call, "Hello,
kids!" from her drive.

Of course, we all wanted to see Elvira first.
"Ooooh, hi, cutie!" Mary Anne said, scooping
her up.

The kids squealed about how cute Elvira is.
And it's true. She's a scrawny little bundle of hair
and knees and elbows, with a pointy chin and big,
big eyes.

"Are you kids hungry?" Mrs Stone asked.

"Yeah!" cried Myriah and Jamie.

"Is peanut butter and jam all right?"

"*Yeah*!" (See what I mean about Mrs Stone
being nice?)

She returned a few minutes later with a platter
stacked with all the ingredients for p.b. & j.
sandwiches.

"Thank you," I said as she put it down on her
picnic table. I found a plastic knife and got to
work.

54

Behind me, three different-sized dogs wandered around the garden, along with a fat goose. "Who's that?" I asked.

"Glynis," Mrs Stone said. "She thinks she's a dog."

"Oh," I said with a laugh. I could tell the kids were in heaven. Myriah was heading towards the Stones' small pasture, where they keep four cows. Jamie was peeping into the pig pen. Mathew and Johnny were—

"Oh! Oh! Oh! Oh!"

That was Jenny, by the barn. Elvira was trying to get behind her. She seemed determined to butt her in the bottom.

"Help! Help!" Jenny cried.

Mary Anne and I both rushed to her, but Mrs Stone got there first. "Bad girl!" she said, pulling Elvira away by the collar.

Jenny was bawling. "I want to go *home*!"

"Darling, have you got anything in your back pocket?" Mrs Stone asked.

"Waaahh! No!" Jenny cried.

I suddenly realized what had happened. Elvira had smelled the squashed egg on Jenny's trousers.

"Here, doggie! Here, doggie!" Johnny was chasing after Mrs Stone's Labrador retriever with a stick.

"Johnny," I said, "put the stick d—"

ROWWWRF! The dog lunged at Johnny. Johnny screamed and jumped away, bumping into Mathew. Mathew tripped over Glynis the goose. Glynis let out a honk, spread her wings, and ran towards Charlotte.

Charlotte turned chalk white. "Aaagh!"

I ran to Charlotte and gave her a hug (Glynis was walking around as if nothing had happened). Mary Anne was holding Jenny up off the ground, comforting her. Mrs Stone was in the barn, putting Elvira into her pen. Mathew and Johnny were rubbing their wounds. And Myriah and Jamie were holding their stomachs, laughing.

"It's not *funny*," Johnny said.

"Uh, why don't we have a snack?" I suggested.

We sat on the picnic bench. Mrs Stone returned and said, "Don't you worry. Elvira's in her pen. The other animals won't hurt you."

"Thank you, Mrs Stone," I said.

We wandered round a little more after our snack. No major tragedy occurred, until Jamie offered the half-empty peanut butter jar to Elvira. She plunged her snout right in, and it got stuck.

With a sharp fling, she sent the jar across the barn.

CRASSSSSH! It smashed into pieces on the stone floor.

"Beeeeeaahh!" Elvira complained.

"It's okay, that's easily cleaned!" Mrs Stone called out.

I couldn't believe how cheerful she was. But I

knew the cheerfulness wasn't going to last forever.

Neither Mary Anne nor I wanted to wait around until it ran out. We politely thanked her and walked back home with our campers.

When the day finally ended, Mary Anne and I collapsed on the front lawn.

"What a day!" was my gross understatement.

"Only four more after this," Mary Anne said.

We both sighed and looked away.

Finally I spoke up. "You know, we really should plan some special activity for our last day."

Then I thought of a sleepover I had organized once. It had been a fundraiser for some pen pals of the elementary school kids, and everyone had had a great time. "Why don't we have an overnight, under the stars?"

"Are you serious?" Mary Anne said. "It's hard enough to control the kids when it's still light."

"We don't have to do anything special," I said. "Can you imagine how cute they'd be—in their sleeping bags with their little pj's."

"Yeah, but it would be a lot of work."

I could tell Mary Anne was beginning to like the idea. And I was convinced it was perfect.

But I didn't want to push it. "Well," I said, watching the sun set, "at least it's something to think about."

6th CHAPTER

Kristy

Tuesday

Dear Stacey,

Remember how great I said practice was going? Well, forget it. Now it stinks.

Everybody's dropping out! It is so frustrating! I don't even know if we'll have enough team members to play the Bashers!

And I will not forfeit the game to Bart Taylor. NO WAY, JOSE.

Even if I have to recruit Boo-Boo to play.

Details later. Miss you.

Kristy the Krushed Krusher

Boo-Boo is Watson's cat. I wasn't being serious.

But I thought about it.

Boy, was I steaming. I mean, we had been practising two or three times a week. Everybody was excited about the game with the Bashers. The team was looking great.

Then, a couple of weeks ago, I received a postcard from Hannie Papadakis, saying she and Linny had to drop out. Okay. At full strength, we have twenty players. But we had lost five of them—Nicky, Claire, Margo, Buddy, and Suzi—to Sea City. Hannie and Linny made seven.

So as of the weekend, there were still thirteen players left for Friday's showdown. You only need nine to play, so we were in fine shape.

Or so I thought.

On Saturday the Gianellis called from their summer house in the Berkshires. Mrs Gianelli was going to stay there all week, selling houses. Bobby and Alicia were having such a great time, they wanted to stay with her. Bobby is the newest member of our team.

Twelve players.

On Sunday I saw Haley Braddock. She reminded me of something I'd forgotten. Her brother Matt was leaving the next day for his special camp for the hearing impaired (he's been deaf since birth). Matt is our best hitter.

Eleven.

Then, on Monday, Mrs Rodowsky phoned.

Jackie had scratched his eye with a plastic drinking straw. Nothing too serious, but he had to wear a patch and would be very sensitive to light for a few days. He *might* be able to play on Friday, but he'd still have to wear the patch. On the left side. Jackie's a righty, so *left* is the side that faces the pitcher when the ball comes.

Now, I don't mean to be cruel to Jackie. I really do love him. But wherever he goes, an accident seems to follow. His nickname is "the Walking Disaster"—and that's with two normal eyes. I couldn't *imagine* what he'd be like with one eye.

Ten.

Still a team, with one to spare.

These were the brave souls who had stuck it out: the Kuhn kids, Jake (eight), Laurel (six), and Patsy (five); Myriah Perkins and her sister Gabbie (five and two and a half); Jamie Newton and Nina Marshall (both four); my brother David Michael (seven); and my stepsiblings, Karen (seven) and Andrew (four).

All ten showed up at our Tuesday practice at Stoneybrook Elementary School. (SES has been really nice about letting us use their playground all year.) As usual, some of the parents decided to stick around. As they climbed into the stands, I called out, "Okay, Krushers, who are we going to beat on Friday?"

"The Bashers!" they screamed.

"Who?" I said.

"The Bashers!"

"All *right*! That's more like it. Now let's have hitting practice!"

Jake Kuhn looked confused. "Shouldn't we wait for the others?"

"There are no others," I said. I explained what had happened, and said, "See, it's in our hands now."

"Oh," Jake muttered. Now he seemed worried and nervous. He looked into the stands, where his mum was sitting.

Jake's slightly overweight, and he's self-conscious about it. It's not unusual for him to have an anxiety attack. I realized I was putting too much pressure on him. "Don't worry, you'll be great," I reassured him.

"How can we play a practice game with only ten people?" David Michael asked. "That's only five on a side."

"We won't," I said. "We'll hit and catch and field, and then we'll play Round Robin."

Round Robin is another idea of mine. Nine players take the field and one goes to bat. Everyone else sits on the bench. If the batter gets a hit, he or she runs the bases as far as possible. Then, when the play is dead, everybody rotates. The batter becomes the centre fielder, the right fielder becomes the centre fielder, and so on. The pitcher goes to the bench and a new player gets to bat.

(Okay, you can stop yawning now. I've finished.)

Anyway, the practice went pretty well. We had a few problems, though. In Round Robin, Nina Marshall hit the ball so far she went around the bases twice. I had to convince her that you can't score two runs in one turn at bat. Gabbie Perkins, who's so little that we have to use special rules (like pitching her a tennis ball instead of a softball), got hit on the head on a slow chopper to second base, but she was all right.

I couldn't help but notice that Jake wasn't his old self. It wasn't until practice ended that I found out why.

As I packed up, I could see him whining about something to his mum. I minded my own business until I heard him say, "Can't we at least go on *Saturday*?"

"Jake, you know what the weekend traffic is like," his mum replied. "I'm taking a day off from work especially to do this . . ."

Uh-oh.

I saw Laurel and Patsy playing catch by the first-base line. Casually I approached them and asked, "Um, when are you going on holiday?"

"This weekend," Laurel answered.

"Which day are you leaving?"

They looked at me blankly. Then they looked at each other. Then they shrugged.

"Mummy?" Patsy finally yelled. "What day are we leaving for Nantucket?"

"Friday morning," Mrs Kuhn called back.

"Nooo!" Jake insisted, stamping his foot.

But Mrs Kuhn had *Yes* in her eyes.

And I had to subtract three from ten.

We were sunk.

As I packed our stuff, I thought furiously. I had to find a solution to this. Who could I recruit? Which of our charges had shown any interest in sports? What about kids I'd never sat for?

A voice interrupted my thoughts. The last voice I wanted to hear.

"Hey, are you lot getting ready to be bashed?"

Bart Taylor was walking towards the field, grinning.

Okay, I said I would tell you about Bart. Here are the most important things to know: He is seriously cute. He has deep brown eyes. His smile is a little crooked, and his hair looks naturally as if he's just stepped out of a salon. He's athletic, too, and he's got a fantastic sense of humour.

All right, he's perfect. Well, almost. He can be really competitive—but then again, so am I. Anyway, he's the only boy I've ever *liked*.

And . . . he likes me!

I'm amazed that we stay friends, when I think about it. The Bashers are the only team we play, and they're older and bigger than we are. But the

Krushers have beaten them, so our rivalry is *intense*.

And until Tuesday, I was sure we'd beat them again.

"Can I walk home with you lot?" he asked.

"Okay." I gathered my siblings together, and the four of us headed towards my house.

When I told Bart about our player shortage, he became very serious. "That's too bad," he said. "It really feels lousy to lose a game. When I was—"

I stopped walking. "What?"

"We lost once when I was in T-ball. Our coach came down with—"

"What do you mean, *lose*?" I snapped.

Bart shrugged. "Well, you can't play with only seven kids on your team, and if you can't play—"

"I'll have a full team by Friday," I said firmly.

"How?"

I looked him straight in the eye. Kristy Thomas was not going down without a fight. "Just watch."

In my old neighbourhood, where Claudia lives, the houses are close together. Everyone knows each other.

Now I live in a neighbourhood full of "top-out-of-sights". That's what Watson calls the people around us, because you can't see some of the houses from the road (they're at the ends of long drives that wind uphill). Many of the kids go to private school or boarding school. So there were quite a few I'd never met.

But most of them were home for the summer. And that evening, I went looking for them.

With bat, ball, and clipboard in hand.

First I walked up one of the driveways to a modern-looking, wooden house.

DING-DING-DING-DONG-DI-DING-DING-DONNNNG!!

Brother! The doorbell played a symphony. That would drive me mad.

I heard rumbling footsteps. The door opened. I expected to see someone like Lurch from the Addams family.

Yea! It was a kid. I thought he looked about seven.

"Hi, I'm a neighbour of yours, Kristy Thomas. Do you like playing softball?"

The boy squinted at me. Then he turned and shouted, "Mum! Collection for Little Lea—"

"No!" I interrupted. I explained about the Krushers and asked if he were interested.

"But I'm in Challengers," he said.

"What?"

"You know, they pick you up on Saturdays and take you to the playing field in Stamford."

I decided Challengers must be some kind of fancy Little League for "top-out-of-sighters".

"Well, I'm offering you the chance to hone

65

your skills *before* Saturday, with a real live championship game. Now, what's your name?"

"Phil Fields, but—"

I wrote his name down. When I looked up, a woman was standing at the door, holding out a five-dollar bill. "Here you go, dear," she said. "And good luck with the season."

It took forever to explain about the Krushers. When I left, Phil and his mum were giving me a weird look.

I went to the next house, which *was* visible from the road. The youngest person there was about eighty-five.

I finally found another kid two houses away. Her name was Kate Munson, and she was mortified at my suggestion.

"But I—I don't know how to play," she stammered.

I smiled. "Nobody else does either! See, you're *perfect* for the team."

"But then how can you have a game if—?"

"Well, I mean, they *didn't* know how, until I showed them how easy it is. Here, hold this bat."

I gave Kate a lesson. Right there on her doorstep. She was awful. Swinging the bat made her scared, so she'd let go, sending it through the air. I thought she was going to break her basement window.

But I could tell she liked playing. I wrote down her name and number.

Then there was S. Emerson Pinckney IV, "Quad" for short (don't ask me why). He probably weighed as much as half my team. And he came to the door with a Nintendo joystick in his hand. I tried my hardest, but it was a lost cause. He did have a younger brother, though, who seemed to hang on to my every word. His name was "Moon" (short for P. Archibald). He was also . . . well, moonshaped.

Next was Sheila Nofziger. You could have fitted four of her into one Quad. She could barely lift the bat, but she was the most excited of all.

I went on until dark. In the end, I thought I could count on about six people—Kate, Moon, Sheila, and three others named Richard Owen, Kyle Abou-Sabh, and Alexandra DeLonge.

None of them had ever played softball. But they were going to learn.

And they were going to play on Friday, or my name wasn't Kristy Thomas.

7th
CHAPTER

MARGO

WENDSDAY

DEAR CAROLYN,
    GEUSS WHAT I FOUND TODAY? A TIDDAL
POOL! I CALLED IT A BEACH ZOO. THERE
WERE SO MANY CRETURES IN IT LIKE CRABS
AND CLAMES AND TENY FISHES 'IT WAS A
GRAT OPPURTUNTY FOR PEOPLE TO LERN
ABOUT MAUREEN LIFE. NOW ITS SUPPER. IM
ABOUT TO EAT A HOTDOG AND SOME COLD
SLAW AND THEN WATSH IT DOWN WITH SALTWATER.
JUST KIDDING !!!!!! BY !!!!!!
                LOVE ALWAYS FOREVER.
        MARGO THE ZOO KEEPER

I love the beach so much.

One of my favourite things is taking long walks. You can see the best sand castles that way. Sometimes you can watch seagulls swooping down into the water and coming up with fish. You can also see them swooping down into dustbins and coming up with rubbish, but that's disgusting.

In Sea City I saw all kinds of cool creatures. One time I found something that looked like a plastic bag filled with water. I stooped to pick it up, but Mal was with me and she shouted, "Don't!"

It turned out it was a *poisonous* jellyfish. Ugh!

I saw lots of clams. I didn't even know that the gross stuff inside it is actually its body. I saw one open and close. And I saw a kind that actually *spits* out water. Once, Mal and I walked out on a jetty, and we saw blowfish swimming in the water. They looked like balloons, but Mal said they could be poisonous.

On Wednesday, Jessi, Claire, and I went for a great nature walk. We were catching sand crabs in a bucket (we always let them go), and I noticed these tiny birds. After a wave came, they would follow the edge of the water back to the ocean. They'd peck-peck-peck with their beaks. Then, when the next wave came, they'd run away!

"What are those?" I asked Jessi.

"Sandpipers, I think," she said.

"Why do they go back and forth like that," I asked, "if they're so afraid of the water?"

Jessi shrugged. "I don't know. Maybe they pick up little bits of algae from the water as it washes back."

I asked Mum later on and she said Jessi was right. Jessi is so clever.

"What's algae?" Claire asked.

"Tiny little plants you can't see," Jessi replied.

"*I* can see them!" Claire insisted. She ran to the water, just like the sandpipers. She crouched low to look for algae. And she ran away when the sandpipers ran.

"Aaaaaaah!"

Claire was not a sandpiper. The wave crashed around her legs and she got scared. She stopped looking for algae.

Further along, just past a jetty, the beach changed. The sand formed a cliff near the water. The waves would crash, then roll *juuust* up to the cliff. Every few feet there were these pools. Some were tiny but some were the size of a small car.

"Ooh, tidal pools!" Jessi said.

"Look!" I cried. One of the pools had creatures in it!

We ran to it. Claire screamed.

In the centre of the pool was a huge, ugly crab. It looked like a helmet with a tail.

"That's a horseshoe crab," Jessi said.

"Is it dangerous?" Claire asked.

Jessi nodded. "I think so. If you step on one."

Claire and I crouched down to look, but we stayed pretty far back.

The pool was amazing. Around the horseshoe crab were a starfish, some snails, sand crabs, and a school of teeny black fish.

"Wow!" Claire said.

The starfish wriggled a little. That made the sand crab crawl sideways. The fish swam back and forth. The snails just sat there.

Then the horseshoe crab moved.

We ran away. But when we looked back, we could see it had barely gone anywhere. I s'pose it didn't really want to leave the water.

"Horseshoe crab-silly-billy-goo-goo!" Claire yelled.

Jessi and I burst out laughing.

"This is soooooo cool," I said. "They're all trapped. The water's like a cage, because the fish can't escape. If they did, they would dry up and die."

"Mm-hm," Jessi agreed.

"It's like a zoo," I went on. "A *beach* zoo."

"Yeah!" Claire said.

A beach zoo. What a great idea.

"I want everybody to see my beach zoo," I said. "We could put up a sign and charge admission."

"Admission?" Jessi looked at me as if I were insane.

71

"Yeah. Come on!"

I ran all the way home. In the living room I found an empty cardboard box we'd packed stuff in. "Can I use this?" I called out.

Dad stuck his head out of the kitchen. "Sure. What are you going to do with it?"

"Make a sign."

I ripped off one side of the box (with Dad's help). Then I ran to my room and found a black marker and some tape.

In no time I had finished my sign. It looked like this:

COME TO MARGO'S!
SPECTAKTULER!!
BEACH ZOO!!!
SEE EXCOTIC AND DANGERUS SPESHIS OF
MAUREEN LIFE !!!!!
ONLY. $50 CENTS

My dad came in and looked over my shoulder. "What's a beach zoo?"

I told him, and he said, "I'll get your mum."

I hurried outside. On the porch was a green shovel with a long handle. It was perfect. I carefully taped the sign to it, using *lots* of tape.

I could see Jessi and Claire by the water, with my brothers and sisters and the Barretts. I marched down there, holding my sign high. "Everybody come to the beach zoo!" I shouted.

"Beach zoo! Beach zoo! Silly-billy-goo-goo!" Claire shouted.

Jordan groaned. "You sound like Va*ness*a!"

Vanessa was building a sand castle with Buddy. She picked up a gloopy handful of wet sand and ran after Jordan.

Adam, Byron, Suzi, Jessi, and Mal followed me. Stacey promised she'd come later, after Buddy had finished his castle.

When we reached the tidal pool, I stuck the spade in the sand. My sign was standing straight up.

"Cool!" Adam said, crouching to see the horseshoe crab.

I stood in front of the zoo and held out my hand. "Only fifty cents for the experience of a lifetime."

"What?" Adam stood up and made a face. "Why should I pay *you*? I can see this for free! This is a public beach!"

"Adam . . ." Mal warned.

"Well, it's true, right, Byron?" Adam said.

"Yeah," Byron replied, trying to peer around me.

Adam turned away. "Let's go."

Byron followed him, then Suzi.

"Sorry, Margo," Mallory said.

"Tell the others the zoo is open," I said.

"Okay."

Jessi was the only one who stayed with me. I

73

stood on the cliff. "Come to Margo's Beach Zoo!" I announced. "Only fifty cents."

Some people on blankets looked over but didn't get up.

A grey-haired couple walked by and peered over the cliff. They just smiled and kept walking.

Some stupid kid ran past and tried to *step* in the beach zoo, but Jessi chased him away. She should have let him get bitten by the horseshoe crab.

Soon Mum and Dad arrived with Mrs Barrett. They each paid their admission fee—and they *loved* the zoo! Dad even turned the horseshoe crab over. It was gross, with all these claws around a small hole (Dad said it was its mouth).

I stayed there the rest of the afternoon. I noticed the waves starting to come closer and closer to the pool.

Then Jessi and I saw a family put their blanket down. They had three kids. I told them about the zoo and they *all* came to see it!

Their oldest boy, George, reached the cliff first. He looked over and asked, "Where is it?"

"Right th—" I began.

But the waves were crashing against the edge of the cliff. The starfish, the snails, the sand crabs, and the fish were all gone.

As the waves went back, we could see the horseshoe crab. It was slowly trying to crawl to the water.

My sign was floating beside it.

8th CHAPTER

Jessi

Thursday

Dear Becca,

Every day there's a new adventure down here. Now it's building sand castles! That's all anyone wants to do. There's going to be a big contest next week. And from what I've seen, Sea City must be the Official Olympic City of Sand Castles.

Give Squirt a kiss and a long tickle from me!

Love,
Jessi

75

"Ice creeeeeam . . ."

"Ice creeeeeam . . ."

"Ice creeeeeam . . ."

"Ice creeeeeam . . ."

Four boys wearing white aprons were singing in front of Ice-Cream Palace. They were probably high school age, maybe college. I think they were supposed to be a barbershop quartet. The last boy who sang "Ice cream" had a voice like a high squawk. His neck veins stood out and his face turned bright red. He looked ready to explode.

But the singers were really good.

Claire, Margo, and Suzi stood in front of them with their mouths hanging open. If I didn't know them better, I'd think they'd forgotten about their ice cream.

It had taken us a while to get to Ice-Cream Palace. The Sea City main street is full of distractions. In fact, it's like one *long* distraction. There are souvenir shops, sweet shops, a miniature golf course, and a place of every bad-for-you food imaginable. Like these:

Kotton Kandy Korner (why kan't they just spell the words korrectly?)

Hercules' Hot Dogs.

Toffee 'n' Things

Burger Garden

Pizza Falafel (I think they mean pizza *and* falafel)

And my personal favourite, Chilli Fotorama

(do they put your snapshots *in* the chilli or on the side?)

Of course, we had walked into almost every one of those places on the way to Ice-Cream Palace. But the Pikes and Mrs Barrett had given me just enough money for cones. That was a wise idea, but it didn't make the trip easy for me.

I was constantly saying things like, "Are you *sure* you want toffee instead of ice cream?"

Anyway, the barbershop quartet finally reached the end of the song. For a flourish they reached into their apron pockets, took out metal ice cream scoops, thrust them in the air and shouted (what else?) "Ice Cream!"

A big crowd had gathered. We all applauded. The boys bowed and ran inside—and we all went in after them.

The four singers scurried behind the counter, ready to serve customers. The one with the deepest voice was very cute. He also happened to be an African-American, which didn't hurt. "Hi," he said. "Can I help you?"

"I want Rocky Road!" Margo blurted out.

"Pistachio Moustachio!" Claire shouted with a giggle.

"Chorcolate!" Suzi said.

"*Chor*colate?" I repeated.

Suzi smiled. "That's how Goofy says it!"

"How many scoops?" the cute boy asked.

77

"Two!" (Suzi.)

"Four!" (Margo.)

"Seven!" (Claire.)

"Whoa, I only have enough for one scoop for each of you," I said.

Triple moans and groans.

"Don't worry, I give big scoops," the boy said.

He was right. The kids walked out with little mountains of ice cream. (I had ordered a vanilla frozen yoghurt. I was determined not to feel like a blob when I returned to ballet class after the holiday.)

On the way home, we passed by Pizza Falafel. On its counter, which faced the boardwalk, someone was buying a falafel plate. It looked like fried meatballs covered with a yummy-smelling sauce. "What's that?" Margo asked the counter man.

"Fried mashed chickpeas!" the man answered cheerfully.

The girls hurried away.

"Ooh, can we play miniature golf?" Suzi asked.

"Too *hard*!" Claire said. (According to Mal, Claire practically set a record for the most strokes per hole at Fred's Putt Putt.)

"Oooh, can we go in one of those?" Margo pointed to a small, wheeled, wicker carriage that

78

was being pushed by a muscular boy. An elderly couple was sitting on the seat.

"Uh, maybe another time," I replied, imagining the puddles of ice cream between the wicker strands.

"Look! Look! Come here!" Now Suzi had plastered her face to a souvenir shop window. In it was a smiling, stuffed toy seagull, wearing a bib that said SEA CITY.

"Aw, he's *cute*!" cried Margo.

(He wasn't.) "Um, I don't have enough to—"

"I just want to *look*. Please please please please!"

"Oh, okay."

The girls stormed into the shop. Suzi ran to the seagull and hugged it. She called it Scuttle, after the seagull in *The Little Mermaid*. Claire was fingering the chocolate bars at the sweets counter, and Margo had her eye on one of those little snow globes.

The saleswoman was very nice. She gave each of the girls a pencil with Sea City stamped on it—for free.

The girls were ecstatic. I felt guilty because we weren't going to spend any money there.

On the way out, I glanced at a big noticeboard outside the shop. I saw a sign advertising a travelling circus on Sunday. When I read that aloud, the kids were determined to go. But another sign was even more interesting:

79

FIRST ANNUAL SEA CITY SAND CASTLE CONTEST!

Wednesday afternoon, west of the jetty
Anyone may enter
Prizes in ALL categories!

"Yea!" Suzi screamed. "Let's all enter!"

"We're *great* at building castles!" Claire said.

You should have seen the girls. They jumped around so much I thought they'd lose what was left of their cones.

"Okay, when do you want to start practising?" I asked.

"*NOW*!"

It was unanimous. The girls wolfed down their cones and ran towards the water.

In minutes I was helping them build castles. They were good, too. Suzi was especially skilled with wet sand. She could take a fistful and let it ooze out, making weird, gloopy shapes.

We worked for a long time. We built a moat, a drawbridge, and a lookout tower. Claire tried to make a troll under the drawbridge, but it looked more like a stalagmite.

As we were finishing up, Mal came over with the triplets, who were tossing a football around. Jordan was sucking on the last part of a Fudgsicle.

"Hey, pretty good," he said when he saw our castle.

"We're going to win the sand castle competition," Margo announced proudly.

I thought Jordan was going to choke on his Fudgsicle. "What? You think you're going to enter the sand castle contest?"

"We don't *think*," Margo snapped.

"I know you don't," Jordan said.

Margo stuck out her tongue. I stood up and took Jordan aside. "Come on, Jordan—" I began.

"Have you seen the other castles?" Jordan asked.

"What other castles?"

"Down there." He pointed towards the jetty. I could see people doing *something* in the sand. "Come on, I'll show you."

Mal agreed to keep an eye on the girls. Jordan and I walked towards the jetty.

As we got closer, my jaw dropped open. The people I'd seen were building castles.

Castles? These were medieval villages— kingdoms! I half expected horses to come out of them.

The builders were mostly grown-ups, and they were working in teams. They were using special moulds and carving tools. One group was even using sand bricks! The detail was amazing— plastic windows and doors, wooden drawbridges that *worked*, real flags flying from the towers,

81

different-coloured sand (is there such a thing as *sand dye*?)

"Oh, boy . . ." I murmured.

"I told you," Jordan said.

The girls' castle was nothing compared to these. But I didn't want to insult them by saying they shouldn't enter.

So far, my week had been great. I'd been a perfect mother's helper, just as I'd wanted to be. But this was going to be trouble. Feelings were going to be hurt.

I had no idea what to do.

9th CHAPTER

Mary Anne

Friday

Dear Mallory,
   We did it! We actually had our mini-camp sleepover! And boy, was it a night to remember. We camped out, played games, and told stories. And ... we may have had a visit from a ghost!
                        Love,
                        Mary Anne
P.S. Don't be scared. The ghost part isn't true (I don't think).

Mary Anne

I don't know how Dawn convinced me to hold an outdoor sleepover.

I'm not the type of person who likes camping. I prefer a nice, soft bed with a roof over my head and air conditioning.

Anyway, we decided to hold it on Thursday night, the night before the last day of Mini-Camp. It would be in the barn if it rained, outside if the weather was nice. We called all the parents and got permission. Everybody loved the idea except the Prezziosos. They didn't think it was appropriate for their angel to be roughing it. But they changed their minds when Jenny threw a tantrum.

Thursday evening was cloudy. Dawn and I prepared for an outdoor campout, hoping it wouldn't rain. We had bought marshmallows, digestive biscuits, and chocolate bars for snacks. (We had had a barbecue for dinner, so Dad and Sharon said we could use the glowing coals.) We set out several huge blankets, then rolled out sleeping bags for Marilyn and Carolyn, who didn't have them.

Jenny was the first to arrive. Her dad brought her over. She was wearing pink slippers and pj's with unicorns on them. She was also clutching a ragged red doll that had been patched a million times.

"She won't go to sleep without it," Mr Prezzioso said in an apologetic voice. He put

84

down the fluffiest, most expensive-looking kid's sleeping bag I had ever seen. Rolled up with it was a foam rubber pad. "She likes a soft sleeping surface."

Marilyn and Carolyn, who couldn't come to the Stones' farm, came next. Then the Hobart brothers, then Charlotte. Myriah and Jamie arrived last.

They were adorable! Mathew and Johnny wore pj's, but Jamie had slipper socks on. "So my feet won't get dirty if I have to get up during the night," he explained.

After the parents had left, the kids rolled out their sleeping bags on the blankets. Charlotte began to look very worried about something. "Um, Dawn?" she asked. "What happens if we . . . you know, if we have to . . ."

"Go pee-pee!" Johnny announced.

"You can use the toilet in the house," Dawn said. "Or . . . go outside, if you want."

That made the campers explode with giggles.

"Who wants to play games?" I asked.

"*ME*!"

Our garden is perfect for running around, so we played Red Light, Green Light; Freeze Tag; and some other games, until it got too dark to see.

Then it was time for snacks!

We sat around the grill. By that time the coals were almost dead, but they did soften the marshmallows a little. Dawn had brought out some

85

sesame sticks for herself (*un*toasted, of course)—
and *those* caught on, too. She had to run inside
and get a whole bagful.

Things were going just great, until I began
hearing a *psssss . . . psssss* noise.

Mathew heard it, too. "What's that?"

"Maybe it's a ghost," Jenny said.

Jamie's eyes popped open. "Um, I want to go
home."

Pssss . . .

Then I felt something. A drop. It was starting
to rain. "You know what that noise is?" I said.
"Raindrops hitting the coals. I hate to say it, but
we have to move this campout inside the barn."

"Then it's a camp*in*, not a campout," Carolyn
said.

We scooped up the sleeping bags and dragged
them to the barn. I turned on the light. "Spread
them out on the hay," I suggested.

After we'd set everything up again, I could see
some yawning faces. And some sad ones. Like
Jamie's.

"What's up?" I said, kneeling beside him.

"I—I just . . . I mimamandadee," he
mumbled.

"You what?"

In the teeniest voice, he said, "I miss my
mummy and daddy."

I put my arm around him. "I know how you
feel. And you don't have to stay if you don't want

86

to. I thought we'd tell a few bedtime stories, and then if you still want to go, my dad can take you home."

I could see a flicker of interest in Jamie's eyes when I mentioned bedtime stories. "Can you tell a scary one?" he asked.

"You *want* a scary story?"

He nodded. "With monsters!"

"Dragons!" Mathew added.

"Worms!" Johnny shouted.

"Worms?" Jenny repeated. "That's stupid."

"No, giant, slimy blood-sucking ones!" Johnny said.

Jenny made a face. Ugh!"

"How about a ghost story?" Charlotte asked.

"Great idea!" Dawn said. "In fact, there may be a ghost, right on this land."

Charlotte smiled and settled into a pile of hay. Jamie, Myriah, and Johnny stared at Dawn, wide-eyed. Carolyn and Mathew looked sceptical. Marilyn giggled and said, "You're kidding."

"It's true," Dawn said. "Or at least some people think it is. You see, almost two hundred years ago, this house belonged to the Mullray family. But they ran into some trouble, and Old Man Mullray had to move the family to Vermont. Well, two of his children went, but his youngest son, Jared, refused to leave. On the morning of the move, when the bank officials came to claim the property, Old Man Mullray called for his son, and they all heard Jared answer, 'I ain't leaving!'

"But the voice wasn't coming from the house, or the barn. It seemed to be coming from somewhere in between. No one ever found Jared Mullray, and to this day, some people think he's still rattling around."

"R-r-really?" Jamie asked.

"I've heard that story before," Jenny said.

"Ah, but you've never heard of Priscilla Gatlin, Jared's fiancee," Dawn said.

Jenny shook her head. The kids leaned forward.

I gave Dawn a Look (*I* had never heard of Priscilla Gatlin).

"Priscilla was madly in love with Jared. But her father was a common blacksmith whose business had fallen on hard times. Old Man Mullray wouldn't hear of the marriage. He thought a move to Vermont would solve his son's crush on this unworthy girl.

"After the old man moved away, Priscilla would visit the farm. She would just sit on the porch, always waiting. Waiting and hoping that Jared would come for her.

"But months went by and he never did. Soon another man in town, Obadiah Spooner, took a liking to Priscilla. One day he followed her when she came to this house. He sat on the porch and

88

said the sweetest things to her. But Priscilla had her heart set on Jared and no one else.

"Then one day it happened. Jared came back. Or at least his voice did.

"Priscilla was sitting on the porch with Obadiah again. This time Obadiah was asking for her hand in marriage. And poor Priscilla, even though she still loved Jared, was tempted to say yes. Obadiah was a wealthy man, and although he had a wart in the middle of his nose, he was kind. Every time he visited Priscilla, he made sure his black hair was brushed handsomely.

"Before Priscilla could answer Obadiah, a muffled voice called, 'Come to the barn . . . come to the barn . . .'

"Well, Priscilla sat straight up. She forgot about Obadiah. The voice belonged to her beloved Jared! She raced to the barn—*this* barn. She flung open the door—"

Dawn fell silent.

"What happened?" Myriah said, her voice a squeak.

Dawn took a deep breath. "The barn was pitch-black. Obadiah called after her, 'Priscilla, stop! No!' But there was no keeping her from her true love. Priscilla walked in.

"Then there was a scream—followed by silence. Obadiah took out his gun and ran into the barn. Shots were fired, *Bang! Bang!*

"Neighbours came running. No one was

foolish enough to go inside, so they waited . . . and waited . . ."

"Then what?" Jamie asked.

"Only one person came out. It was a man with hair as white as snow, sticking straight into the air. His eyes were wide open and glassy, as if he'd seen something no man was supposed to see. No one recognized him until he came closer. Then they could see the wart on the nose."

"Obadiah!" Charlotte said.

"Yes. He noticed no one as he walked out. He went straight to his house, lay down on his bed and never again got up, although he lived a good twenty years more. The neighbours went into the barn then, but no one else was inside. Not Priscilla, not Jared. Not a trace. Some say Jared was alive, and took her to Alaska to marry him. Others say the ghost killed Priscilla. Still others say that Priscilla, too, became a ghost, and to this day she walks the barn, looking for Jared."

The only sound in the barn was the tapping of rain on the roof. The kids were openmouthed. I could see Dawn reaching towards the trap door (there actually is a secret passageway that leads from the barn to the house). But I gave her a sharp Look. If she opened that door, no one would sleep that night.

Including me.

Just to be safe, I stood up and rolled a lawn mower over the trap door.

"I think they're both still alive," Carolyn whispered.

"If they went to Alaska, maybe they turned into Santa and Mrs Claus," Johnny said.

Charlotte yawned. So did I. "Listen, everyone, it's getting late now. What do you say—" I was going to suggest lights out, but that didn't seem like such a great idea. "—we go to sleep?"

There weren't any protests. One by one, everyone began to nod off. "Good job," I whispered to Dawn. "Where'd you hear that?"

She shrugged. "I made it up."

"Fantastic!"

I put my head down. It *was* a good story—and a good sleepover. But I had a hard time falling asleep.

I couldn't keep my eyes off the lawn mower.

10th CHAPTER

Claudia

Friday

Dear Stacey,
 Im about to leave for my last day
of sumer school. I cant balieve I
actualy feel sad. (just a little) Wierd,
huh? The kids turned out to be prety
nice. Oh well, by the time this card
gets to you, I will be in Sea City! And
I will read it and probly wonder
how I coud have felt anything but
extatic!   Cant Wait!!!! (really)
        Claud

"Good morning, class."

It had been twenty long, long days. And old Mrs Wegmann had begun each one with the same highly original greeting. For twenty days, the fluorescent strip light above the left side of the room had given off the same annoying buzz. For twenty days, I had been counting backwards from twenty.

Now I was at One. At long last, the Summer of Torture was ending.

I should have been thrilled. Thrilled? I should have been dancing on my desk. I'd got decent grades. Good enough so that I was guaranteed to pass even if I failed the final exam. All I had to do was sit there and not commit a crime. When the bell rang, I would be ready for G-M-O-O-H:

Get Me Out Of Here!

And then I could start thinking about serious things. Like which bikinis to take to Sea City.

"Well, here we are, our last day," Mrs Wegmann droned on. (Duh, no kidding!) "I'll give you some time for questions, then we'll have our final exam."

You know what? Four kids asked questions, and I knew the answers to each one! Me, Claudia "The Brainy One" Kishi, budding maths genius!

The test began. There were a few tough problems, but mostly they weren't too bad. I even managed to finish a bit early, believe it or not.

While I was waiting for the official end, I

93

looked around the class (not too obviously, so Mrs Wegmann wouldn't think I was cheating).

Carly's tongue was hanging out of her mouth—and she was *chewing* on it. *Very* suave. I wanted to giggle and tell her.

I looked at the clock. Two minutes till the end of summer school. Feelings began rising up inside me. Half of me wanted to celebrate, but the other half felt a little sad. I would miss my new friends.

Don't get me wrong. If I had had one more day of summer maths lessons—one more *hour*—I think I would have passed out.

But still . . .

BRRIIIINNNG!

"Class, have a wonderful rest of the summer!" Mrs Wegmann shouted over the cheering.

We ran out of the room, throwing our papers on her desk. Out in the corridor, Carly practically started screaming. "We did it! We did it!"

Theresa shouted, "We are officially *not* stupid!"

We gave each other a big hug and danced around.

"Speak for yourself," grumbled another classmate, named Fran. "I think I'm going to have to repeat this stuff again."

"Oh, Fran, no you won't," Carly said. "You passed the quizzes, right?"

"Most of them," Fran answered.

"Okay, look," I said. "What answer did you

get on the word problem about the doughnut bakery?"

As we discussed the test, Fran began feeling better. A lot of our answers were the same.

We walked together through the front door of the school. As we waited for the bus to arrive, we started feeling nostalgic.

"Remember the day Mrs Wegmann had the hiccups?" Theresa asked.

"And the time David Gabel called her Mrs Wigwam?" Carly piped up.

Another classmate, Barbara, grinned at me. "And the quiz you thought you'd brought your calculator to, but it was your VCR remote control?"

We all howled.

"I'm going to miss you lot," Carly said sadly.

"Oh!" Theresa blurted. "What are you all doing on Sunday?"

Everyone said "Nothing," except me. I told them about Sea City. Just *mentioning* it made me feel wonderful, until Theresa spoke up again: "Because my mum and dad said I could have an end-of-school barbecue for us."

"I can go," Carly said.

"Me too," Fran and Barbara added.

My heart sank. I really wanted to go to that party. But I was supposed to leave with Mrs Barrett's boyfriend and his kids on Saturday. Maybe I could tell him I'd stay and take a bus on Monday—

Stay? Was I crazy? I'd only been looking forward to this for a whole summer!

A school bus roared up to the front door, which meant Barbara and Theresa had to leave.

" 'Bye, Claudia!" they said. "We'll miss you!"

"Me too!" I replied.

"Write, okay?" Barbara said.

"I will!"

We hugged, and promised to keep in touch. Theresa said she'd have another party at the beginning of school.

They climbed in. We kept shouting " 'Bye!" to each other through the open windows.

Carly, Fran, and I walked home. Fran's house was closest to the high school and mine was next. At each one we had a long, tearful goodbye.

At home, I ran straight to my room to start packing. I felt *much* less excited than I had expected. In fact, when Dawn and Mary Anne came by to visit, the first thing Mary Anne said was, "Are you okay?"

"Yeah, fine," I replied.

"Want to go to the Krushers game with us?" Dawn asked.

"It's actually happening?" I said.

Mary Anne nodded. "You know Kristy. She managed to put a team together at the last minute."

"This I have to see." I pulled a suitcase out of my wardrobe and opened it up.

Inside were three bags of crisps. I'd forgotten all about them.

So . . . we snacked while we packed.

Mary Anne and Dawn told me about the famous Mini-Camp overnight. Mary Anne said she had woken up in the middle of the night to a noise.

"I could have sworn it was a female voice," she said, "calling out, 'Carrot! Carrot!' I thought Charlotte was calling for her dog in her sleep." (Carrot is the name of Charlotte's schnauzer.)

I shrugged. "Was she?"

"No," Mary Anne replied solemnly. "She was fast asleep. But I know who the voice belonged to. It was the ghost of Priscilla Gatlin, saying, '*Jared! Jared!*' "

"Oh, stop!" I could feel myself shivering.

Dawn laughed. "Mary Anne woke me up. Then she went back to sleep—and *I* couldn't sleep. Then Jamie woke up whining. I thought he was having a ghost dream, too, but he just had to go to the toilet."

Our conversation turned to Sea City. We talked about the postcards we'd received. We gabbed away until I was all packed. By that time I was fully, totally, one hundred per cent excited about Sea City.

And I couldn't wait to see Kristy's new Krushers.

11th CHAPTER

Kristy

Friday

Hi, Sam!
How's camp? Do you like being a counselor? I hope you have a VCR there. If you do, go to the nearest town and rent <u>The Bad News Bears</u>.
Multiply that by ten. Then you'll have an idea of what the Krushers' championship game with the Bashers was like.
Your frazzled sister,
Kristy

"Come on, pitcher!" Kyle Abou-Sabh shouted. He cocked his bat, ready to smack a practice line drive.

"Kyle, that's first base," I said. "Home base is to your left."

I gently pushed him in the right direction.

Moon Pinckney was already at home base, doing some warm-up swings of his own. He seemed to be getting the hang of it—except for one minor thing.

"Uh, Moon," I said, "take your glove *off* when you bat."

"Oh," he replied.

As he removed his glove, I noticed something else. "And when you *do* wear it, it goes on your right hand, not your left."

"But I'm a lefty," he said.

"Exactly," I replied. "You'll be able to leave your left hand free to throw. Besides, look where the thumb is."

I left Moon staring at his mitt.

Kate Munson was playing catch with Myriah Perkins near the third-base line. Myriah was pitching very gently to her.

And Kate was ducking each throw as if it were a hand grenade.

Richard Owen had brought a tennis ball to the game and looked confused.

Alexandra DeLonge had come dressed in a brand-new designer baseball outfit. She was

99

trying desperately to wipe a smudge of dust off her right ankle. In the stands, her parents and grandparents were having a champagne picnic and toasting each other.

Sheila Nofziger was picking dandelions in left field.

"Let's look lively, everybody!" I shouted. "The Bashers will be coming any minute!"

Actually, the Bashers weren't due for another half hour, but we were in dire need of some serious practice.

I had got a team together, all right. But what a team. Our only hope was that the Bashers would be laughing so hard they'd pass out and lose the game.

I'm exaggerating. I was much more optimistic than that. For one thing, we hadn't lost any more Krushers that week. We still had seven original members. If I kept them all in the game, that meant only two of my new people had to play at any one time. (Of course, I'd rotate them so they'd all have a chance to play.)

Alexandra wasn't a bad catcher. And I could put the other new player in right field, where he or she couldn't do much harm. (Why? Because most batters tend to hit to the opposite field: righties to left field and vice versa. So, since most batters are righties, not too many balls are hit to right field. That's a bit of Kristy Thomas Baseball Wisdom, and you heard it here first, folks.)

100

When the Bashers did arrive, Bart stood by the batting cage and watched the end of our practice. I tried not to talk to him, but he tracked me down.

"Are you sure you don't want to cancel?" he asked.

"Not on your life," I said. "We're here, aren't we?"

"Kristy, look, you don't have to lose, okay? We can just drop the game—or postpone it."

I smiled and shook my head. "I'm not a quitter, Bart."

He took off his cap, looked out to the field, and scratched his head. "Okay. But, uh, maybe you should tell your outfielders to stop playing patty-cake."

Sure enough, Sheila and Kate were playing some hand-clapping game in midfield. As Bart walked away, I ran to them and said it was time to play ball.

Sheila looked surprised. "Oh, drat!" she complained, skulking away.

Oh, drat? Why did she think we were all here?

The Bashers, being bigger and older, held a very short practice. A very short and *disciplined* practice. Honestly, I don't know why Bart ever organized this team. His players could join Little League or T-ball, no trouble.

Moon was staring at them, goggle-eyed. "W-we're playing *them*?" he whispered.

"Hey, we've beaten them before," I said in the most confident voice I could manage.

Then it was time to begin. The remaining BSC members had turned up. They were in the stands, cheering and looking, well, *dubious*.

Watson had agreed to be the home base umpire. Even though Watson's obviously a Krushers fan, Bart hadn't protested a bit. (I think he knew we needed all the help we could get.)

Bart and I met with Watson at the pitcher's mound. We agreed to play seven innings. Then Watson tossed a quarter and I won the toss. We would take the field first.

Our pitcher was Marilyn Arnold. Alexandra was behind the base, as backstop. Kyle was in right field, looking lost. Another questionable player was at second base. David Michael was our shortstop, so I hoped he'd be able to handle anything hit to the infield.

The first Basher batter stepped up. He wore a confident smile. He took a few practice swings, so hard you could hear the wind swoosh.

Bart shouted, "Take it to right field!"

Now Kyle looked terrified.

I closed my eyes and prayed.

"Ball one!" Watson called out.

"New pitcher new pitcher new pitcher!" one of the Bashers kept repeating.

"Knock it off!" David Michael yelled. "You're boring!"

"Ball two!" Watson barked.

"Come on, get it over the base!" the batter taunted.

Marilyn walked him on four pitches. He sauntered to first base, spitting every few feet, as if he were a pro.

"Keep cool, Marilyn, you're looking good," I said. (Okay, so I was lying.)

The next batter hit the ball between second and third. David Michael scooped it up. He turned to throw to second.

Our second baseperson was drawing a happy face in the dirt. "Look up!" David Michael screamed.

Too late.

The ball hit second base and bounced into right field.

Kyle froze. He pointed to himself, as if to say, "Me?"

"Throw it to third, Kyle!" I yelled.

Kyle squatted, waiting for the ball to come to him. It rolled between his legs. He bent down to watch, like an ostrich just before it buries its head.

"Go and get it!" I called out.

He ran after it, picked it up, and threw with all his might. Richard Owen made a perfect catch.

Unfortunately, Richard Owen was sitting on the bench.

Both batters were jumping on home plate. "Inside-the-park home run!" they squealed.

"Unh-uh," I protested. "Interference from the sidelines. That's a ground-rule double!"

"Ask the referee," Bart said calmly.

I looked at Watson. He smiled and shrugged. "Sorry, the runners crossed homebase before Richard touched the ball."

"Two to nothing!" the first batter gloated.

"You *lot*," Alexandra groaned. "Why don't you watch where you're going!"

She was standing behind homebase, dusting off her trousers. The runners had kicked up a cloud of earth around her.

"Can I call half-time, to change?" Alexandra asked Watson.

"Oh, brother . . ." I muttered to myself.

I closed my eyes and sat on the bench. This was going to be a long game.

The final score was 34—1, Bashers. Our one run came when Gabbie whacked her tennis ball past the Bashers pitcher, who had moved in close. The third baseman picked up the ball and threw it so hard it sailed into the stands, and my older brother Charlie hid it.

Gabbie skipped around the bases and scored. Even the Bashers cheered her.

After the game, no one seemed particularly crushed. Some of my new players even seemed proud of themselves—which was great. I

congratulated them on their play and comp-
limented them to their parents.

Claudia, Dawn, Mary Anne, and Watson all
tried to tell me what a phenomenal job I'd done.

Inside, however, I felt as if I'd just tried to
move a boulder up a hill by blowing on it with a
straw.

I was tired. But I was proud we hadn't given
up.

Bart found me later and said, "Good game.
Have fun in Sea City."

I think I answered him, but I can't remember
what I said.

I walked home from the game with David
Michael, Karen, and Andrew. Karen looked
upset.

"It's okay," I told her. "We did the best we
could, and we had fun."

"I know," she said. "It's just that . . . that . . ."

"What?"

She sighed. "Well, Nannie and I baked a
victory cake for you, Kristy. It was supposed to be
a surprise. It says 'Congratulations, Coach,' on
it—and we *lost!*"

"That's so sweet, Karen!" I said. "I don't care
what it says. It's the thought that counts."

We walked on in silence. But just before we
reached the house, Karen's face lit up. "See you!"
she said, and she raced inside.

David Michael, Andrew, and I walked into

a living room decorated with streamers and balloons. "Surprise!" Mum and Watson called out.

A few minutes later Nannie and Karen came in from the kitchen. Karen was proudly holding a cake. The icing looked smudged, but the letters were clear enough.

They said GOODBYE COACH!

"We're going to miss you, Kristy," Karen said.

I had been so busy with the Krushers, I'd almost forgotten about Sea City. I was leaving the next day!

I suddenly felt much happier.

"Oh, thanks, you lot," I said. "I'll miss you, too."

My "victory" party? Well, it turned into the nicest farewell celebration I could imagine.

12th CHAPTER

Stacey

saturday

Dear Charlotte,

Well, the Babysitters Club is together once again. Yea! We had so much fun catching up. The weather was incredible today, too.

But not for long. Guess what? We may be in the middle of a huge hurricane soon! And there's a lady nearby who looks like Miss Gulch— and she rides a bike. Wee-dee-dee-dee, wee-dee-dee-dee (Twilight Zone theme). At least we aren't going to have a tornado.

See you in a week — if I'm not in the Emerald City!

Luv always,
Your almost sister,
Stacey

107

"AAAAAAAAAGGGGGHHHHHH!"

No, that was not the cry of the Wicked Witch of the West as she melted.

It was the happy screaming of seven Baby-sitters Club members. (Well, there were eight of us, but Logan managed to confine his jubilation to a boyish smile.)

Claudia, Dawn, Kristy, Mary Anne, and Logan had arrived with Mrs Barrett's boyfriend, Franklin Harris. He has four kids from a previous marriage: Lindsey (who's eight), Taylor (six), Madeleine (four), and Ryan (two).

Ten people in a van! No wonder they looked so happy to be out.

The conversation sounded like this:

"We had such a . . ."

". . . feels so good . . ."

". . . Mini-Camp . . ."

". . . six new players . . ."

". . . I missed you . . ."

". . . me too . . ."

". . . Rosebud . . ."

". . . summer school . . ."

". . . Elvira . . ."

". . . you should have seen . . ."

Finally Kristy stuck her fingers in her mouth and let out a loud whistle. "Okay, let's get settled first! Then we can catch up!"

Once a chairman, always a chairman.

108

The Pikes had worked out sleeping arrangements with Mrs Barrett. Dawn would stay at the Barretts' to look after Franklin's kids. Logan, Kristy, Claudia, and Mary Anne would stay at the Pikes'. On Monday night, Logan would go back to Stoneybrook with Franklin and his gang (Logan had to work on Tuesday), and then Dawn would move to the Pikes'.

I wasn't thrilled about the last part. I sort of wished Mrs Barrett would say, "Oh, the Pikes' house is so crowded. Surely Dawn can stay with us!"

Uh-uh, no way, didn't even think of it.

Well, that was understandable, I suppose. After all, Dawn had been invited by the Pikes in the first place.

Dawn and I ran upstairs to my room. A camp bed was there, and I had set it up for her.

"We're roommates!" Dawn squealed, plopping her suitcase on the bed.

"Yeah!" I squealed back.

Dawn pulled a swimsuit out of her suitcase and began changing. "Tell me everything, Stacey. Claudia told me you saw Toby. And he acted as if nothing had happened."

I sighed. "Yeah. What a dork. I just said, 'Hit the road, Jack. You're blocking my sunlight.' "

Dawn screamed. "No! You *didn't*."

"You're right. I didn't. But I was really cold to

109

him. And you know what that creep did? He started flirting with Mallory!"

"*Mallory*? No! Seriously?"

"Seriously. She and I haven't been talking much."

"Has he asked her out?"

"Oh my lord, no! She'd have told me *that*! Besides, he's not interested in her. She's only eleven."

We gossiped for a few more minutes. I told her a little about how difficult Mrs Barrett had been, but I didn't go into details. It was midday, and I'd promised Mrs Barrett we'd take the kids to the beach.

We gathered up the kids and trooped next door to the Pikes'. Everybody was ready, and Kristy began lining us up in front of the porch as if we were in a race.

"Come on, take your positions," she ordered us.

"*Kristyyyyy*," Dawn said.

"On your marks . . ."

Dawn and I sighed. Buddy and his sisters thought this was a great idea. So did Franklin's kids.

"Get set . . . GO!"

Kristy, Claudia, Mary Anne, Jessi, Mal, Nicky, Margo, Vanessa, Claire, Buddy, Suzi, Marnie, Lindsey, Taylor, Madeleine, Ryan, Dawn, and I all began running. Sand flew

110

everywhere. Our charges shrieked with joy. Then I shrieked. Then Dawn. Then everyone else— including Mary Anne.

Logan was already on the beach, playing Frisbee with the triplets. The boys stared at us as if we were a landing of alien invaders.

I didn't care. We were all here. It was the happiest I'd felt in a week!

In case we were wondering whether Kristy's Idea Power diminished outside Stoneybrook, we found out that day.

It didn't.

Somehow Kristy had devised a way to convince the grown-ups to take the kids for half an hour. From five-thirty to six. Do you know why?

You guessed it. A Babysitters Club meeting!

Without phones, without records, without subs. The best kind.

We gathered in the Pikes' kitchen, still in our swimsuits. The wind was whipping in from the sea, through the screen door. We wrapped our towels around us.

Mal had decided to change before the meeting. When she walked into the kitchen, she saw an empty chair between Jessi and me.

She decided to stand near the doorway. (Which, to be honest, was okay with me.)

A radio was droning on the windowsill. As we gabbed away, Kristy shushed us.

111

"*. . . low pressure system moving in tonight, the lows in the upper fifties. This is WCCT, Sea City. The time at the tone will be five-thirty. . . .*"

At the sound of the *beeeeep*, Kristy pounded her fist on the table. "I call this meeting to order!"

A plastic salt shaker clattered to the floor.

Claudia rolled her eyes. "Puh-leeze, Kristy."

"I hereby declare a special emergency gossip session of the Babysitters Club," Kristy went on.

We cheered.

"First, a report from the chairman regarding the Krushers' heartbreaking loss!"

Kristy told us every detail of her game. Then Claudia described her new summer school pals and cracked us up with an imitation of her teacher. Dawn and Mary Anne talked about Mini-Camp and the sleepover. Then us Sea Cityers told of our adventures down here.

I hadn't laughed so hard in a long, long time. We were *gasping*.

I couldn't help but notice that Logan didn't say much. He looked pretty tired. I thought he might have felt left out, so I asked, "How's your job, Logan? Do you still like it?"

He shrugged. "It's okay, I suppose. Hard work, though."

That was it from the male camp. Oh, well. I thought he must be too exhausted to say much. Or maybe the job was boring.

In the conversation's lull, we could hear the radio again:

"*. . . we have a report now that Tropical Storm Bill is picking up speed and moving northwest, about four hundred miles off the coast of Jamaica. It's too early to tell what will happen, but if it continues in its current path it could become the first major hurricane of the year . . .*"

"Wow," Jessi said. "I'm glad we're not in Jamaica."

I'd never been in a hurricane. I wondered if it was like a tornado. I started thinking about *The Wizard of Oz*.

Then Claudia remembered another funny story about summer school. Kristy turned the radio off, and we began laughing our heads off again.

13th CHAPTER

LOGAN

SATURDAY

HEY, KERRY AND HUNTER!

YOU TWO HAVE TO SEE THIS PLACE.
YOU WOULD LOVE IT. MARY ANNE AND I
TOOK A WALK ON THE BOARDWALK
TONIGHT. THERE'S EVERYTHING—
INCLUDING THIS MONSTER FERRIS
WHEEL AND MILES OF ARCADE GAMES.

I WISH I COULD STAY HERE MUCH
LONGER. TOO BAD I HAVE TO GO
BACK TO THE ROAD SPUD. OH, WELL,
SEE YOU MONDAY, AND DON'T DRIVE
MUM AND DAD CRAZY WHILE I'M
GONE!

YOUR COMMANDER-IN-CHIEF,
GENERAL LOGAN

114

The Road Spud is my nickname for the Rosebud Cafe. Actually, I didn't make it up. It's kind of a tradition to call it that. You can say it and no one realizes you're making fun of the name.

But enough of that. That's another story.

Anyway, there I was in Sea City. I was really happy to see Mary Anne. I was not happy to be the only male among the entire Babysitters Club for two whole days—but I could deal with that.

I mean, the BSC members are some of my best friends. They're nice and funny and clever. They're just not boys (duh, bet you didn't know that). Which means when I'm in a room with them, they sometimes feel they can't talk normally to each other.

Do you know what it's like to be surrounded by seven girls who love to yak but can't go all out? It's awkward. Awkward? I break into a sweat that feels like a monster slimed my shirt collar.

But to tell you the truth, things were pretty cool at Sea City. Everyone seemed relaxed in our impromptu kitchen meeting. There was hardly any giggling-with-hands-over-mouths or funny looks at me and Mary Anne.

I have to admit I was thinking of something else. Just slightly. You see, Mary Anne met this boy called Alex down here.

Now I don't want you to think I'm a raving jealous type. I'm really not. Besides, Mary Anne told me they were only friends, and I believe her.

115

And Alex supposedly has a girlfriend back home. But I don't know. Sea City is a romantic place, and Mary Anne and Alex went out to eat together and stuff, and just the idea that she and he were enjoying a holiday here while I was in Stoney-brook. . . .

Well, what can I say? I'm human. It bugged me.

But only a bit.

After the BSC meeting, Mary Anne and I went for a walk along the beach. It was cool outside, like autumn, which meant Mary Anne snuggled up close to me, which I liked a lot.

"Logan, it feels so good to be here with *you*," she said.

"Yeah," I answered. "Do you miss being a mother's helper?"

She snuggled closer and smiled. "Not now."

We passed about fifty yards' worth of monster sand castles. I saw some incredibly complex stuff, but that work seemed like such a waste. I mean, it's *sand*. Sooner or later it all has to come down.

Just beyond the sand castles was a jetty. Beyond that was a group of kids playing. Two boys, of about our age, were looking after them.

"Hi!" Mary Anne shouted.

The kids turned round. So did the two boys. They grinned when they saw us.

Mary Anne ran excitedly towards them. I followed, at a slower pace.

116

The kids eagerly showed Mary Anne their castles and holes.

When I reached them, Mary Anne said, "Logan, this is Toby and this is Alex."

"Hey, how's it going?" Toby said.

"What's up?" Alex asked. "Mary Anne told me all about you."

Both were still grinning. They stuck out their hands and I shook them.

So this was Alex.

He was pretty good-looking, I noticed. I wouldn't cast him in a teen heart-throb film, but as looks go, his were solid.

Mary Anne took my arm and squeezed close to me.

"Pretty cool out tonight," I said.

(Well, I had to say something.)

"Brrrrrr," Mary Anne agreed, holding me tighter.

I got the feeling Mary Anne wanted to make *sure* Alex knew I was her boyfriend.

"Yeah," Alex said. "Well, just as long as we don't get hit by Bill."

It took me a minute to realize he meant the tropical storm.

We fell silent then, just kind of smiling and nodding and shifting weight. Then one of the kids called out, "Alex, look at my maze!"

"Well, nice meeting you!" Alex said. "Got to go!"

117

Everyone said goodbye. Mary Anne and I turned and walked back to the Pikes'.

And that was that. I think Mary Anne was nervous, but I felt fine. I mean, it was no big deal. There's no law that says a guy's girlfriend must *never* have any male friends.

Anyway, I was bigger than him.

Alex wasn't mentioned for the rest of the evening. I made sure of it. I didn't want to blow up anything that really wasn't important.

Dinner at the Pikes' was a madhouse. We cooked up eight pounds of hamburger meat and twenty-seven hot dogs.

Afterwards, Mary Anne and I had an actual date on the boardwalk. What a place! We took a long romantic stroll . . . until I saw bumper cars.

"We have to go on these!" I said.

So we did. Then we played arcade games. Then I won a stuffed penguin for Mary Anne at Hoopla—and she won a pair of (cheap) sunglasses for me.

We ate some homemade fudge, then some homemade candy floss, then took a ride on the Ferris wheel (which was *almost* not a good idea after eating so much).

I felt like a kid again. Sea City was even more fantastic than I had expected. Mary Anne and I didn't stop laughing. I felt so close to her.

And that was when I started thinking about

guess who. I know it was ridiculous, but I couldn't help it. Okay. If I were a boy, a *friend* of Mary Anne's, and we decided, hey, let's go on a *friendly* walk, maybe ride the Ferris wheel, have a cone, visit the arcade, watch the sunset on the water.... Do you get the idea? I mean, you'd have to be made of cardboard not to feel all warm and lovey-dovey inside.

Wouldn't you?

I tried to put it out of my mind. I dragged Mary Anne to the Ghost Train. (That took some bargaining. I had to promise to watch the glassblower afterwards.) On the way there, we heard some tourists saying, "Do they dismantle the rides during a hurricane?"

That made me laugh. "Isn't it amazing?" I said. "This tropical storm is a thousand miles away, making up its mind where to go—"

"I know," Mary Anne said. "And people are so sure it's heading straight for Sea City."

We stood in line and prepared for something *really* spooky. To be honest, I don't care much for ghost train-type rides. But the Tunnel of Luv was closed for repairs, so this was the next best thing.

Mary Anne looked scared. That made me smile. At least I could be reasonably sure she hadn't gone in there with—well, anyone else.

14th CHAPTER

Mallory

Saturday

Dear Mrs. McGillicuddy,

Just kidding about the name! Remember, from "I <u>love</u> Lucy"? Anyway, your daughter is a fabulous mother's helper. The Barrett kids really love Stacey! Today was the best of all. Everyone arrived from Stoney- brook. We're taking over! They're thinking of changing the town's name to BSC City! Just kidding again. Bye!

Love, Mallory

P.S. Mum and Dad send their love.

There were some things I couldn't tell Mrs McGill in my postcard. Like how rude her daughter was being. And how wonderful that day really was.

It started out pretty typically. Beach, lunch, more beach. But Margo and Nicky got bored, so I took them into Sea City for a couple of hours.

Every few metres along the boardwalk are these binoculars, perched on swivelling posts. For a quarter, you can gaze around for about two minutes.

Nicky and Margo both wanted turns. I let them use two neighbouring binoculars. "I can see a kid changing *outside*!" Nicky yelled.

"Oh, yeah?" Margo replied. "Well, I can see a shark."

"You can? Where?"

"You can only see it on this one."

"Oh, go and wash your head in bubble gum." Nicky swung his binoculars around to look at Margo. "Ugh! Ugh! I can see a slimy, snaggle-faced blubberfish!"

Margo pulled her face away from the binoculars and looked at Nicky. "Where? . . . Oh, you little—*Mallory*! He called me a—something bad."

I decided to change the subject. "Hey, who wants to go into town to play miniature golf?"

"Me!" they both shouted.

I don't know why I said that. The moment the

words left my mouth, I regretted them. The last time the Pikes played miniature golf, we made half of Sea City furious with us for taking so many strokes to get through the course.

Oh, well, with only three of us it might not be so bad.

We left the boardwalk. When we reached the main street, Nicky called out, "Look! Gurber Garden! Can we go in?"

"But we've already eaten," I replied.

"Just to *look*," Margo said, as if going to look at the inside of a hamburger place were something *everybody* did. The "Gurber Garden" was actually Claire's name for a restaurant called "Burger Garden".

"Yup, they still have that secret delicious orange sauce," Nicky the gourmet remarked when we were inside. "Mustard mixed with ketchup. They do the work *for* you."

When we came out, we saw a clown juggling on the boardwalk. He was wearing a sandwich board that said DIXIE BROTHERS CIRCUS. "Come to the circus this Sunday!" he shouted. "One day only!"

"Ooooh, can we go? Please!" the kids asked.

"We have to ask Mum and Dad," I told them. "Now, come on!"

Next stop was Fred's Putt-Putt Course. I half expected our faces to be plastered to the walls of the rental place, like WANTED posters, reading: DO NOT RENT TO THESE PEOPLE.

But all I saw was a Sea City Savings Bank calendar and a list of prices. I rented three putt-putt clubs, and we were off.

There was a line, not too long, made up mostly of kids. (Thank goodness. Maybe we wouldn't be the slowest ones.)

As we drew closer to the rental desk, a couple of the little boys in the queue began to look familiar. They turned around at the sound of a voice behind us saying, "No Coke, just 7Up and Dr Pepper!"

I spun round. Standing at a drinks machine, almost hidden by the rental building, was Toby.

"Dr Pepper!" one of the boys called out.

"Me too!" the other one said.

"Can we get Dr Peppers, too? Pleeeeeease?" Margo asked.

"Sure!" I said.

What a great idea. I was happy to go to the machine.

As I walked to it, I said, "Hi." (Not original, I know.)

"Oh, hi, uh—wait, don't tell me . . . *Mallory*!" Toby said.

He remembered! "Right . . . Toby," I replied.

"Hey, we're batting a thousand! Can I get your drinks? I have lots of quarters."

"No, that's okay," I said.

I noticed Toby had two Dr Peppers and one 7Up. I made sure to get the same.

While I was putting the money in, he *waited* for me. He waited to walk me back to the queue!

I mean, it was only about twenty steps, but still I could tell Toby was a sweet boy.

Toby's charges, Ben and Peter, were eight and six years old. They'd already met Nicky and Margo at the beach. The four kids were blabbering away like old friends.

"Hey, we're next for rentals," Toby said.

"Uh-huh," I replied.

"Why don't we do this together?"

"Okay."

I was dying for him to ask me something that wasn't a yes-or-no question. I was sure he thought I was a total no-brain.

But I had nothing to worry about. We spent a long, long afternoon together. Well, not really *together*, because Toby spent a lot of time helping Ben and Peter with their technique. (Boys can be very competitive, even at miniature golf.) Nicky and Margo kept looking at them, trying to imitate everything Toby was doing.

Me? I'm a pretty good golfer, if I do say so myself. I just played quietly, and helped the kids if they asked.

Toby would smile at me once in a while and wink. It always, always made me blush. Which I *hate.* I have red hair and freckles to begin with, so I look like a ripe, hairy tomato when I blush.

When we were at the "Old King Cole Hole", Toby said, "Have you taken lessons or something?"

"No," I answered, ripening again. "I just aim and hit."

He crouched next to me, imitating my stance. "Now, let's see, your shoulders are like this, right?"

We talked a lot. The kids played well—but cheated a lot, which was all right because it made the game go faster.

At the end, we all walked home together. Ben and Peter insisted on playing leap frog with Margo and Nicky.

Toby and I couldn't help laughing. "Kids are a handful," Toby said.

I rolled my eyes. "Try living with seven of them—brothers and sisters, I mean."

Toby let out a low whistle. "It must be mayhem. Do your parents give you a break—like, time off from helpering?"

I shrugged. "They do, if I ask."

"Oh. Well, would you like to *ask* about Friday evening?"

For a moment the words just hung in the air. I felt as if I were walking around them. Looking at them. Making sure they were the ones I had heard. Making sure I knew their meaning.

Then my stomach did a flip-flop. Toby was asking me out! Wasn't he?

"Um, Friday evening?" My voice sounded as if I'd just swallowed some helium.

"Yeah. I have the evening off. And I wasn't planning anything, so I thought maybe you and I could . . . you know, go out. If you want."

Yes! *Yes! YES*! He *was* asking!

My mouth answered before my brain could think another thought. "Well, sure, Toby. I'd love to!"

"Great! I'll pick you up at seven at your place?"

"Okay!"

He looked at his watch. "Ugh, I'm late. I have to rush. See you Friday!" He ran off and pulled his charges away from their game.

As they disappeared down the beach, I thought I would just float away with happiness.

"Come on," I managed to say to Margo and Nicky. "Let's change for dinner."

They raced each other to the house. I pinched myself. It wasn't a dream. It had happened.

It felt as if a hummingbird were fluttering around in my heart. I wanted to scream, but too many people were around. So I squeaked. I didn't care who heard me.

I had to tell Jessi.

I flew to the house. I could hear the kids inside

changing. I bounded upstairs, ran straight into the room, and slammed the door.

"Mallory!" Jessi gasped. "You scared me."

I plopped on my bed and said, "Oh, Jessi Jessi Jessi Jessi Jessi Jessi!"

"What what what what what? Are you okay?"

"No." I shook my head and looked her straight in the eye. "I'm in love."

15th CHAPTER

Dawn

Sunday

Dear Mum and Richard,
   Where is the summer?
Today we had to wear jackets!
Boy, were we lucky. We
found something to do
indoors. A circus! And I
don't mean the Pikes'
house.
   This one only had one
ring, and it was much
quieter.
         See you in a week,
                  Dawn

"Agggghhh!"

There was a creature in the bathroom. It was communicating in no language known to human-kind. But one thing was clear. It brought a message of great annoyance.

Suddenly it appeared at my bedroom door. It held up a piece of wet rectangular pink fabric. "The pink one is mine!" it said. "The green one is yours."

It then stormed away to the bathroom.

"I know," I replied.

"Good. Then would you mind wiping your face on *your* towel next time?"

I went to the bathroom. "Stacey, I *did* wipe my face on my towel. Maybe one of the kids used your towel. Don't forget, there are six new people in the house this weekend."

"No kidding. And everyone has decided to wipe their hands and faces on *my* towel."

Oh, boy. Talk about waking up on the wrong side of the bed.

I sighed. Maybe it was the weather. Sunday was cool and grey. Definitely not a beach day.

Moments earlier, Mrs Barrett had stopped by our room. She said she and Franklin wanted to take the kids on a trip to Smithtown, a re-stored Colonial village nearby, if it didn't rain.

The way Stacey was acting, I was glad we'd be

129

away from the house, in a public place. Then *maybe* she'd be on her best behaviour.

What had caused the sea change in Stacey? (Don't you love that expression, "sea change"? Mary Anne's dad uses it to mean a humongous change. I thought it was appropriate here in Sea City.) I knew things weren't going great for Stacey. She'd been a little distant the day before. She'd complained about Mrs Barrett. She'd said she missed being a mother's helper at the Pikes'. And she was *not* pleased when Mallory came home all starry-eyed about Toby. Neither of us could believe he'd asked her out on a date.

Still, I couldn't see how any of these things, especially that last thing, would bother Stacey. She couldn't stand Toby. She'd said so. Often.

"Stace?" I asked, standing in the bathroom doorway. "Are you angry about something besides the towel?"

"No. What should I be angry about?"

She began brushing her teeth furiously.

"Well, I thought maybe you were thinking about . . . you know, Toby and Mallory."

Stacey laughed. The mirror became polka-dotted with flecks of toothpaste. "Are you kidding? She can have him!"

"That's what I thought."

Brush, brush, brush, spit. "He's just going to treat her like a disposable dishrag."

130

"Yeah."

Rinse, rinse, rinse, spit. "I told her, but she wouldn't listen to me."

"I remember."

Gargle, gargle, gargle, spit. "Anyway, I couldn't care less what they do. Now let's go downstairs, before Mrs Barrett has one of her fits."

"Okay."

We dressed quickly and ran downstairs. The kids were already up, which made me feel a little guilty.

"But I don't *want* to go to yucky, boring Smithtown!" Buddy's voice rang out from the kitchen.

Everyone was crowded around the table. Franklin was at the stove making omelettes. And Mrs Barrett was looking annoyed. "How do you know it's boring?" she asked.

"It just *is*!" Suzi chimed in. "Today's Sunday, and that's the day of the Dixie Circus!"

"Yeah, we want to go there!" Lindsey said.

When Franklin saw us, he shouted, "Hey, girls, what do you want in your omelettes? We have cheese, mushrooms, pepperoni, anchovies, prunes, raisins, chicken nuggets, chocolate chips—"

He began dancing around, throwing ingredients in the omelette pan.

"Franklin, stop!" Mrs Barrett said, laughing.

131

Stacey didn't crack a smile.

Despite Franklin's comedy act, the Smithtown versus Dixie Brothers debate continued. Finally, in the middle of breakfast, Mrs Barrett said, "Enough! Franklin, why don't you and I drop the kids off at the circus with Dawn and Stacey. We'll go on to Smithtown and pick them up afterwards. Okay?"

"Yeeeaaaaa!"

A very wise decision had been made. I was actually glad to be going to the circus. I just hoped the Dixie Brothers could pull Stacey out of her bad mood.

Well, I suppose when I had heard the name "Dixie Brothers", I had thought of "Ringling Brothers". I wasn't expecting just a little tent in a vacant car park on the edge of town. Outside the tent were a few rides and concession stands. It was very . . . *temporary* looking.

As we queued to buy tickets, we saw a life-sized statue of a pirate propped up against a tent post. He had a wicked smile and a patch over one eye, and a hairy wart at the end of his nose.

"That is so lifelike," Lindsey said, walking over to it.

"Is it part of the circus?" Buddy asked.

"Sure is!" a clown shouted from behind us.

132

"We just bought it from Madame Trousseau's Wax Museum!"

"Really?" Taylor said. He stepped up close to it, followed by the rest of the kids.

Stacey and I stayed in line. "Don't break it," Stacey warned them.

Buddy touched its costume, then reached towards its face. "I just want to touch its wart!" he said.

Suddenly the statue slapped Buddy's hand away. "Aghhh! Blimey, a mate can't get a rest on dry land around these parts," he snarled.

"AAAAAAGGGHHH!" Buddy, Suzi, Lindsey, Taylor, and Madeleine all screamed and backed away. Ryan and Marnie burst into tears and ran into our arms.

Then, with a smile and a wave, the pirate said, "Top of the mornin' to ya, mates," and walked away.

The clown bounded up to us and patted the two little ones on the head. Then he grinned and said, "Expect the unexpected at the Dixie Brothers!"

As he walked away, his trousers fell down. Instantly, Marnie and Ryan began to giggle.

"He was real all the time!" Lindsey said.

"Yeah, he was tricking us!" Buddy realized.

"A pretty cheap trick, I thought," Stacey said.

We bought our tickets and saw the show. How

133

was it? Well, honestly, not great. There was one ring, and a few tired animals performing tricks. The trapeze act was scary, but mostly because it looked like the flimsy tent was going to fall down. And the sword swallower actually swallowed a flame-tipped sword (I have never worked out how they do that). The clowns were okay, and the pirate walked around and tried to be scary while the clowns kicked him.

From the kids' reaction, you'd have thought we were at the Big Top. They *adored* the show! When it was over, they ran outside and begged us to take them on rides.

As Stacey and I kept an eye on them, I bought us some pretzels. She took one bite of hers and said, "You know what I really want? Some peanuts—the kind that are in their shells."

I didn't really feel like going back to the end of the line at the food stand. But I wanted to make Stacey happy. "You stay here and watch the kids," I said. "I'll get some."

"Thanks, Dawn."

Well, guess what? I couldn't find any peanuts except the sugared, shelled kind. "No luck," I said to Stacey. "I suppose they don't have them here."

Stacey looked at me blankly. "Yes they do. I saw some."

Then *she* went looking. When she came back, her brow was all creased. "I could have sworn I saw people eating some. Oh, this is so depressing. I have *such* a craving."

Stacey began to sulk. I tried to make conversation with her, but it wasn't easy. She seemed really upset about the peanuts.

When Franklin and Mrs Barrett came back, I felt relieved. On the way home, the kids chattered on and on about the circus. I added a thing or two, but Stacey just stared out of the window.

"We heard some exciting news in Smithtown," Franklin said at one point. "Some of the shops in Sea City are stocking up on supplies—bottled water, batteries, tinned food—in case the hurricane hits."

"Why?" Lindsey asked.

"Well, the old-timers remember how the causeway washed out in the last hurricane," Franklin replied.

"Oh, no!" Suzi said.

"Don't worry, sweetheart," Mrs Barrett said with a chuckle. "That was years ago, before they could build strong roads, and before they had big speedboats that could take supplies back and forth."

"Besides," Franklin said, "there's no hurricane anyway, just some storm down near Jamaica. And the weatherman says it's going to be hot and sunny tomorrow, with no clouds."

"A beach day?" Buddy asked.

"Well, yeah," Franklin replied. "For all you lucky Barrett kids."

"Yippeee!"

Me? I was looking forward to the next day, too. I felt as if I'd been babysitting for eight kids that day. Tomorrow the Harrises would leave, and I would move to the Pikes'.

Then I could have a *real* holiday.

16th CHAPTER

Mary Anne

Tuesday

Dear Logan,
    Are you feeling better today than you were yesterday? I hope so. You looked so sad. Not that I was a perfect specimen. I hope I didn't cry too much. I miss you SOOO much!
    I saw Alex and Toby today. They really liked you. (They thought you looked like Cam Geary, too, so there!)

Mary Anne

Oh, guess what? I may be coming home sooner than expected. We may be getting that storm after all.

Love always,
Mary Anne

Poor Logan. On Sunday he had told me a bit about his job at the Rosebud Cafe. He's their youngest waiter, but he's so good that they give him twice as much work to do. Added to that, lunch business is booming. (Probably because of all the girls who turn up just to look at him.)

But we had a great visit. Sea City has become a special place for me, and it was wonderful sharing it with him. I think he had a good time, too. He loved the boardwalk and the beach.

It was funny, though. Sometimes he just wasn't *himself*. He'd go really quiet, which isn't like Logan at all. I thought it might have had something to do with Alex. Logan seemed a bit uncomfortable meeting him.

I asked Logan about his moods. He assured me he was just thinking about having to go back to Stoneybrook on Monday.

Sigh. I certainly knew how he felt. I wished his visit could have lasted a week. I felt *miserable* when he left. As usual, I started blubbering. And as usual, my friends teased me about it. Dawn

138

handed me a tissue, but it got sopping wet. So Kristy handed me a beach towel.

He left about midday with the Harrises. The day was bright and sunny, and we spent the rest of it on the beach. The Big Event was a fight between Buddy and Nicky. They were building a castle together and Nicky was in charge of putting water in the moat.

SPLASH! He dumped in a pailful and went back for more.

"Hey!" Buddy shouted, "You broke the drawbridge!"

Nicky turned round and stared blankly.

"I spent *hours* on that," Buddy went on. "You mend it."

"I didn't mean to break it," Nicky said. "*You* mend it!"

"*You* broke it."

"*You* should have made it stronger!"

"Mend it, Nicky-Nicky-Got-So-Sicky!"

"No, Buddy-Buddy-Elmer-Fuddy!"

Nicky picked up a fistful of sand and threw it in Buddy's face. With an ear-splitting scream, Buddy covered his eyes. "Owww! He got *sand* in my eyes!"

Stacey rushed to Buddy. Mallory rushed to Nicky.

"He started it," Nicky said.

"Ow! Ow! Ow! Ow! It hurts!" Buddy screamed.

139

Stacey calmly walked him into knee-deep water and tried to rinse his eyes. "It's okay. You'll be all right . . ."

Mal gave Nicky a scolding. Then she took him by the hand and walked towards Stacey. "Is he okay?" she called out.

"Fine," Stacey snapped. "Mal, can't you or Jessi keep a closer eye on these kids? They shouldn't throw sand!"

"I'm sorry," Mal said.

"What planet were you on, anyway? Or were you too busy with . . . with fantasies of older boys?"

Whoa. That didn't sound like Stacey. Poor Mallory didn't know what had hit her. I could see her eyes water, so I took her for a long walk.

Later Stacey apologized (thank goodness). Honestly, I didn't know what had got into her.

The next day, Tuesday, started out nice but became cloudy and cool around midday. Buddy, Suzi, Vanessa, Margo, Marnie, and Claire insisted on building sand castles, even in the overcast weather. The triplets and Nicky wanted to go into town and see a double feature of *Robin Hood* and *The Sword in the Stone*.

Mal and Jessi agreed to stay at the beach, and Stacey went to the cinema. She and Mal, needless to say, were barely talking.

As for us "guests"? Kristy and Dawn stayed

140

with the beach crowd, and the rest of us went to the theatre.

Afterwards, as we were gabbing about Prince John's death scene, Claudia said, "Is it Sunday or something?"

"Huh?" I asked.

Claudia pointed to the road. "Look at all these cars."

The street was bumper to bumper. "That's weird," Stacey said. "Maybe a lot of people had four-day weekends."

We didn't give it much more thought, until we returned to the Pikes'. There, Mr and Mrs Pike were sitting in the kitchen with Mrs Barrett. They looked very serious.

"They say the road was strengthened a few years ago," Mrs Barrett was saying.

"They said the *Titanic* was unsinkable," Mr Pike replied.

"Is the *Titanic* going through the marsh?" Claudia asked.

We all cracked up. "No," Mrs Pike said. "We're just talking strategy in case Hurricane Bill hits."

"There *is* going to be a hurricane?" Stacey asked.

Mr Pike shrugged. "Nobody can tell. The storm is gathering force off the coast of Florida, and it's expected to blow north. It could blow out to sea, or just fizzle."

141

"Or it could hit the Jersey coast, right?" Stacey said.

"It could," Mrs Barrett answered. "But if that happened, it wouldn't be until tomorrow night or Thursday morning, at the earliest."

"Shops are stocking up in case we're cut off from the mainland," Mrs Pike added.

"Some people down the road are boarding up their windows," Mr Pike said.

"This'll be great!" Adam blurted out. "We can stay inside, tell stories and eat Spam and tuna fish and fruit cocktail."

"I'm scared," Byron said, standing close to his mum.

"Is a hurricane like a tornado?" Nicky asked.

"No, sweetheart," Mrs Pike said. "It's a very, very windy rainstorm."

"Well, if it is going to come, we should think seriously of going home beforehand," Mrs Barrett suggested.

"The weather people have only called a hurricane *watch*," Mr Pike answered. "That means there's a possibility it'll come. Maybe fifty-fifty, maybe less. A hurricane *warning* means there's a good chance."

Mrs Pike exhaled. "I don't know. It *is* only a *watch*, and we have the house till Saturday. It would be a shame to give it up for nothing."

No one said a thing for a few minutes. Me? I was hoping we'd stay. I agreed with Mrs Pike.

Finally Mrs Barrett said, "I think you're right. It's not worth giving up our holiday for a fifty-fifty chance. We just have to be prepared."

Mr Pike stood up from the table. "Then it's settled. I'll go into town and get some supplies, just in case." He grabbed a pad and pen from near the phone. "Now, what do I need to get? Bottled water, tinned food—"

"Torches and batteries," Mrs Pike said. "Candles, maybe a battery-operated radio and clock—"

"Chocolate and cookies!" Jordan suggested.

"Can I go with you?" Adam asked.

"Me too!" the other boys screamed.

I was starting to feel tingly inside.

This was getting exciting.

17th CHAPTER

Jessi

Wednesday

Dear Mama and
Daddy,
Wish me luck. It
is eight o-clock in
the morning, and
Claire and Margo
have been up for
hours. They are
determined to win
the Sea City Sand
Castle Contest. That
is a little like
Daddy entering the
New York City Ballet
competition planning
to win it (no

*offence, Daddy). The
other contestants are
pros! I think they
plan to live in
their castles year-
round.
Oh, well. I can
handle a few
tearful kids... can't
I? After all, I am
a Super Sitter.*

Love and kisses,
Jessi

This Sitter was not feeling very Super on Wednesday. Especially at six in the morning.

That was when I felt the earthquake. Well, in my dream it was an earthquake. I was dancing on stage with the American Ballet Theater. Suddenly I felt my body bounce around. Then the floor opened up. I looked down and saw the orchestra falling into a big hole. One of the violinists was shouting, "Can we go and make castles now?"

That's when I opened my eyes and saw Claire Pike. She was jumping up and down on my bed. Margo was doing the same, on Mallory's bed.

"Can we?" Claire repeated.

"You sound just like the violinists," I said with a yawn.

"Huh?"

"Never mind." I looked out of the window. It was *dark*. It was also cloudy and cold and gloomy. The kind of morning that makes any normal person want to sleep late.

I plopped back into bed and said, "It's far too early, you two. The contest doesn't begin for four hours. Can't you wait a while?"

"Ohhhhhhh," Margo started to moan.

"Come on," I heard Mallory say. "You can practise in front of the house, okay? Just let us sleep."

"But we've been practising for days!" Margo complained.

"Well . . . go and have breakfast," Mal said. "Do *something*. Just let us sleep."

That worked for a while. Sort of. *Mal* slept. I tried, but I kept thinking of that earthquake. Then I'd hear bumps and giggles downstairs and feel as if I wasn't doing my job.

Finally I went downstairs and helped the kids make their breakfast. Then, while they played outside, I wrote a postcard in the living room.

Before long, the rest of the family was up. I, Super Sitter, went to work. I made pancakes, poured cereal, cleaned up spillages, and washed dishes.

"Jessi, you are amazing," Mrs Pike said at one point.

Boy, was I glad to hear that. I almost forgot how tired I was.

146

When Mal came downstairs to help, things became easier—although Margo and Claire could hardly sit still. Every few minutes, Claire would run inside and ask, "What time is it now?" One of us would answer, for instance, "Eight twenty-seven," and she'd say, "How many more minutes till ten o'clock?"

By nine-thirty I'd had enough. "Okay, Claire and Margo. Let's go for it!"

"Yeeaaaaaa!" Claire screamed.

"We're going to win!" Margo yelled.

I gritted my teeth and tried to smile. I was hoping they'd want to enter the contest for *fun*. I was hoping they weren't serious about "going for gold."

But I was wrong. And I knew I'd have a few broken hearts to mend in a couple of hours.

"Good luck!" Mal said. "I'll bring the others down a bit later."

"Great!" I replied. I stepped outside to see what the weather was like.

Still dreary and chilly. "You two," I said, "go and get your windcheaters." I got mine, too, and we shoved off. Margo and Claire were loaded up with tools—plastic buckets, spades, and a bag full of seashells to use as decorations.

We walked next door to pick up Suzi (Stacey stayed with Buddy and Marnie). Suzi came running out with a shopping bag full of her equipment.

Jessi

Mrs Barrett and Stacey waved goodbye. "I'll come with my camera!" Mrs Barrett shouted.

Fine, I thought. As long as she got pictures of them *before* the results were announced.

We walked towards the north jetty. I had to bundle myself up tightly against the cold. I looked to the horizon, but the sun wasn't peeking in anywhere.

"Aren't you cold?" I asked the girls.

"A bit," Margo said.

"When you start getting wet," I said, "you're really going to feel it."

"That's okay," Claire piped up.

"You're sure you don't want to stay at home, have some hot chocolate, maybe read a story—"

"*No!*" was the unanimous reply.

I gave up. There was no turning back now.

We walked to the lifeguard stand. Two very adorable, muscular boys were standing on it. "Hi," said one of them.

"Hi," I answered. "We came to sign up."

The boys looked at each other, then back at us. "Sign up? You mean, for the castle competition?"

"Yeah!" Margo said.

"Oh, that's been cancelled because of the storm," the second lifeguard said. "They're going to hold it next week—Wednesday, I think."

Margo dropped her equipment in the sand. "Ohhhhhh!" she groaned.

148

"Lifeguard-silly-billy-goo-goo," Claire said under her breath.

"*Yeah*," Suzi agreed, thrusting out her lower lip.

Next week! Whoa, I was saved! We'd be miles away by then.

I looked round. The beach was *empty*. I'd barely noticed. In fact, I'd sort of forgotten about Hurricane Bill, Tropical Storm Bill, or whatever it was.

"So what about some hot chocolate?" I said.

"*Yeah*!" The girls started running back.

You know what I decided? Hurricane or storm, Bill was my hero.

18th CHAPTER

Claudia

wednesday

Dear Carley,
   Oh, I hop this card gets to you. This
hole place is in a panick. You
woldnt belive it its like a film
In fact I'm writting this in the car,
stuck in traffic. Sea city is being
evo~~ku~~ ~~avagdat~~ cleared out because
of the hurrycan.
   Its exiting but scary. What if we
all get blowk away?
   Oh well, if I die, you can have all
my art equiptment!
                        Love always,
                           Claudia
P.S Just jocking dont worry. (I think)

150

Our ears were plastered to the radio. (Wait. Ugh. What an image. Oh, well. You know what I mean.)

"*To repeat, the hurricane watch has become a hurricane warning. The tropical storm is now officially Hurricane Bill. Coastal-flood and small-craft warnings are in effect, for winds up to one hundred miles an hour. Residents are advised to stay away from coastal and outlying areas. All New Jersey beaches are closed. We have reports that Bill is already creating extensive damage along the North Carolina shore and should arrive in New Jersey this evening, after which he will proceed up the East Coast. . . .*"

Mrs Pike turned down the radio. All of us—kids, grown-ups, Barretts, Pikes—were crowded in the kitchen. Outside the rain was already pounding against the window.

"Well," she said, "what do we do now?"

Mr Pike scratched his chin. "We can't stay here. A beach is the worst place to be in a hurricane."

Poor Byron's lower lip was trembling. "Are we going to die?"

Mrs Pike smiled and hugged him tight. "Absolutely, positively not."

(Byron looked happier. I wasn't so convinced.)

"But I'm not so sure it's a great idea to pack up and return home," Mr Pike said.

151

"Darling," Mrs Pike replied, "three days of holiday time is not as important as—"

"I'm not thinking of the holiday," Mr Pike said. "I wonder how clever it is to try to drive to Connecticut. We'll be in the hurricane's path the whole way, in heavy traffic, with no visibility—most of the trip will be at night."

Then Kristy spoke up. "We'd be better off just moving inland, to a motel or something."

Leave it to Kristy. *One* statement, and we have a perfect solution to the Problem of the Year.

"That's a good idea," Mr Pike said. He glanced out of the window, then looked sternly around the room. "Now listen. I want everybody to pack just a few clothes into overnight bags. Enough for two days, at the most. *And I don't want any fighting.* This is very serious. We'll meet back here in fifteen minutes. Now, go."

We went. Fast. I have hardly ever heard quiet, easy-going Mr Pike talk like that.

Kristy and I ran to the room we shared. Kristy threw some underwear, some socks, and a T-shirt into a rucksack. "Come on," she said.

I was having a dilemma. I was wearing the only long trousers I had packed, these overdyed navy jeans. I was also wearing a loose black cotton sweater over a white tank top. So if I packed my big purple Hawaiian shorts, which were the next warmest trousers, I'd be stuck having to wear an *orange* striped shirt, which was the only long-

152

sleeved one I'd brought. Unless I wore the sweater again over it. . . .

"Uh, Claud?" Kristy said. "Bill is a hurricane, you know—not a fashion-show judge."

"I know, I know. You go ahead. I'll be right down."

Clomp-clomp-clomp-clomp. Kristy was the first one downstairs. "Someone should phone Stoneybrook!" I heard her yell.

I ended up packing three outfits—one in case it was cold and rainy, one in case it was warm and rainy, and one really nice one to change into if necessary (or if the weather cleared up). I thought that was very sensible.

Oh, and some extra shoes and a big bag of Mars bars I'd stashed away for a rainy day.

When I got downstairs, everyone's luggage was piled in the kitchen—along with beach equipment and chairs.

Dawn ran inside, soaked. She was carrying two folded-up beach umbrellas. "We're bringing everything inside, so it won't blow away."

In the living room Mr and Mrs Pike were taking down the wicker swing from the porch. "I think this is it," Mrs Pike called out.

"Is there anything else we need to do?" I heard Kristy ask.

"Well, I called Ellen Cooke at the estate agents, and she said to turn off the water supply and the

153

electricity," Mrs Pike said. "And board or tape up the windows."

I had a sinking feeling. There are about a hundred and fifty windows in that house. And the weather was getting worse by the minute.

"I don't think we can worry about the windows now," Mr Pike said. "It looks as if the whole neighbourhood is clearing out, and we're going to hit the major traffic. I'll deal with the electricity. You all get into the cars now."

Aye, aye, Captain Pike! (No, don't worry, I just *thought* that. I didn't say it.)

I took my suitcase and ran outside. It was *pouring*. I could barely open my eyes.

"In here!" Kristy called from the van. I followed her voice and jumped in.

"You sure you packed enough?" she asked as she hauled my suitcase into the back storage area.

I shook myself off and looked around. Mallory and Jessi were in the front seat. Mary Anne, Dawn, Margo, and Claire were squeezed in the middle seat. That left the long back seat for Nicky, Vanessa, Kristy, and me.

I could see Mr Pike running towards the Barretts' estate car. He shouted, "How many do you have?"

Mrs Pike's voice shouted back, "Nine!" (The Barretts and the rest of the Pikes were travelling together.)

Mr Pike climbed into the driver's seat and

counted us. "Eleven!" he shouted out of the window. "Let's move it!"

Vrrrooom! The engine started. I looked at Kristy. A tiny smile was on her face. I could tell she wanted to do just what I wanted to do.

Squeal.

This was very, very exciting.

"Where are we going, Daddy?" Margo asked as we pulled out of the drive.

"I don't know, darling," he said. "The first place on the mainland where we can find somewhere to stay."

Mr Pike drove slooooowly down the street. He put the windscreen wipers on the fastest speed, but they didn't help. The rain drenched the window right after each wipe.

"Can't see a blessed thing," he muttered.

Somehow he found his way into the centre of Sea City. It looked like a ghost town—a soggy ghost town. Most of the shop windows were covered by big wooden boards. Either that or huge X's made of thick tape.

The traffic was very heavy. Horns blared left and right. We slowed to a stop as we approached the causeway.

Soon we could see flashing red lights everywhere.

"What's going on?" Kristy asked.

Mr Pike rolled down the window and stuck out his head. "Here comes a policeman," he said.

We leaned forward to listen. I could feel my heart pounding. Were they letting cars over the causeway one at a time? Had a car spun out and crashed?

"Excuse me!" Mr Pike shouted. "Can you tell me what's happening?"

A policeman in a rain suit and boots appeared by the window. "Causeway's underwater!" He had to yell to be heard over the rain.

"You mean *no one* can leave the island?" Mr Pike said.

"That's right, sir! I'm awaiting further instructions."

He vanished. Mr Pike rolled up the window and sank into his seat.

Vanessa started to cry. "Daddy, are we going to be in a flood?"

"No, sweetheart, they're going to tell us where to go."

"But we're stranded!" Margo said. "The hurricane's going to get us!"

She burst into tears, which made Nicky sob, too.

Oh, my lord. This was not fun at all. My mouth was feeling dry. I wanted to open the door and run. I felt trapped. Another few minutes of this rain and the van was going to turn into an ark. If it didn't sink.

I was about to scream when the policeman ran to the van again. Ahead of us I could see

156

cars moving to the side of the road, making U-turns.

"Sir!" he yelled. "We've been instructed to tell everyone remaining here to take shelter in the junior school. Turn around here and go three blocks to Cottage Road, then turn right. The school's on top of the hill."

"Thanks!" Mr Pike backed the van up and turned round. His eyes were glued to the rearview mirror. "Come on," he mumbled. "Stick with us."

Slowly we inched our way across the town. The rain pounded like war drums on the roof.

Or maybe that was the sound of my own heart.

19th CHAPTER

Stacey

Dear Mum,

I am writing this by torchlight. We are all in the gym of the Sea City Elementary School. I know you must be worried about me. You've probably been hearing about Hurricane Bill, and how the causeway got washed out. Well, we're safe and dry. This building is like a fortress.

I will mail this tomorrow. I heard they're going to send a mail <u>boat</u> to the mainland after the hurricane passes

I love you. Don't worry.
Your stranded daughter,
Stacey

"I can't see the street signs!" Mrs Barrett said, squinting through the front window.

"Just follow the van's tail lights," Mrs Pike said calmly.

"Are . . . are . . . are . . ."

Poor, frightened Suzi was curled up in my lap. Her question was coming out in gasping sobs.

"Are we lost?" she finally asked.

"No, we're almost there," I said reassuringly.

Did I believe that? No way. I was scared out of my mind. I thought we'd never reach the school. I was sure the water would rise up and carry us into the ocean.

To our left, Adam stared glumly out of the window. "This stinks," he grumbled. In the very back of the estate car, Byron and Jordan agreed with him.

Buddy and Marnie were in the front seat, bawling their eyes out. Mrs Pike held Marnie in her lap and gently stroked her hair. Somehow she managed to put her left arm around Buddy's shoulders. "Rain, rain, go away," she began to sing, "come again some other day."

I was very happy Mrs Pike was in the car. I don't know what I'd have done if Mrs Barrett were the only grown-up there. I think she was the only person more scared of the hurricane than I was.

Mrs Barrett steered the car to the right. We began climbing the hill to the school. Next to us, a

159

couple of people were *pushing* a car up the hill. "Ugh, what a time to have engine trouble," Mrs Pike said.

She was trying to sound light-hearted, to make everything seem more normal.

But there was nothing normal about a hurricane. And there was certainly nothing normal about being stranded on an island at sea.

It seemed like hours before we finally approached a car park. It was jammed. "Where on earth are we supposed to park this thing?" Mrs Barrett said.

"I think anywhere's fine. Just pull over to the side of the road. Let's get inside," replied Mrs Pike.

Mrs Barrett did so. We hopped out of the car.

It was like being under attack. It felt as if all the water in the world had been collected in one huge bucket and dumped over Sea City. I was drenched in about two seconds as I ran to the back of the car.

I yanked the door open. "You lot take your stuff and stick close to your mum!" I shouted to the triplets.

As Byron and Jordan scrambled out, I grabbed as many bags as I could. The two mums were herding the rest of the kids out of the car.

"I'm going to take Marnie inside!" Mrs Barrett yelled, scooping her into her arms. "Stacey, you follow me with Buddy and Suzi!"

"Okay!" I replied. I grabbed Suzi's hand. Buddy was right by my side with his rucksack.

"We'll get the rest of the bags!" Mrs Pike shouted.

Nobody was crying now. We needed all our energy just to put one foot in front of the other. The wind was like a big hand trying to push us back down the hill.

Somehow we reached the side door of the school. We stepped inside onto a filthy, wet lino floor. The noise was deafening, between the rain drumming against the windows and the people shouting.

I pulled my hair back and squeezed out as much water as I could. My charges were all with me, safe and sound. That was my first concern. They'd started crying again—but so had about a hundred other kids around us.

Mrs Barrett was hugging Marnie. I crouched down and put my arms around Buddy and Suzi. "We're safe now," I repeated over and over again.

I looked around. We were in a gym. The windows had been boarded up from the outside. Some of the boards were rattling in the wind. At the far end of the gym, people were setting up camp beds with blankets. A small group valiantly tried to mop water off the floor. In the midst of it all, a man in raingear was shouting something into a megaphone.

Pandemonium. Total, utter chaos. No wonder the kids were screaming.

"Remind you of the SES sleepover?"

I looked up to see Dawn smiling at me. Just beyond her were the other members of the BSC and the rest of the Pike family. I felt awfully relieved.

"Yeah," I said, "except ours was noisier!"

Dawn laughed.

"Quiet, please! May I have everybody's attention?" The man with the megaphone was finally managing to be heard over the din. "With the help of the local Red Cross, we are in the process of setting up camp beds. If any of you have dry sleeping bags, it would help us greatly if you'd use them. Now, we have a team of volunteers preparing food in the canteen, which is down the corridor. I can't promise a gourmet meal, but there's ample tinned food for everyone here. And as long as the refrigeration holds out, I believe we have some ice cream for the children!"

Boy, did he know the right thing to say. All those crying kids were suddenly buzzing with excitement.

"So settle down, have some grub, and make some new friends," he continued. "We may be spending quite a bit of time together."

I heard a smattering of applause. The sound level rose again, but not nearly as high. A lot more

162

people were smiling, and many were shaking hands and chatting.

Mr Pike waved us all towards him. "Okay, let's have a strategy meeting."

"I want ice cream!" Claire said.

"I know you do," Mr Pike replied. "We'll go to the canteen as soon as we've found some beds. I see quite a few empties in the far corner, so let's go over there!"

We picked up our bags and ran. In no time we had got a sleeping corner of our own. All the kids (and most of us BSCers) got beds. The grown-ups, Kristy and Mal agreed to sleep on the floor on blankets.

As for dinner, well, it was divine. I had a savoury helping of tinned devilled ham, garnished with canned lima beans (in their own juice). My beverage? A V8 juice cocktail. Topping it off was a stick of sugar-free peppermint gum courtesy of our private confectioner, Claudia Kishi.

I have to admit, there *was* something exciting in the air. The kids were screaming and wolfing down food like mad.

When it was time to head back to the gym, I took Suzi and Marnie's hands. Suzi seemed agitated. "What's up?" I asked.

"I didn't bring my pj's," she mumbled.

"Me neither," Buddy said.

"Me threether," Adam chimed in.

163

"That's okay," I cut in before we got any fourther. (Sorry.) "I think we can sleep in our clothes tonight."

"Yippeeee!" cried the kids. (Isn't it amazing what kids find exciting and fun? Just thinking about sleeping in my clothes made me feel grungy.)

When we were halfway across the gym, the lights went out.

Just like that. No warning, no sound, no electrical *dzzzzit*, nothing.

Everyone in the gym fell silent for a moment. Then I heard some baffled mumbling, then some groans, and people calling out for lost family members.

"Mum?" said Nicky's timid voice.

"Stick together, everyone," Mr Pike said firmly. "Hold hands and follow my voice."

Suddenly about six sets of emergency lights popped on. They cast pools of dull amber light around the gym.

Slowly we made our way to the beds.

"Uh, it looks as if we've lost some power, folks," the man said through the megaphone. "We'll be passing round candles and torches in a moment, so just sit tight."

Fortunately the Pikes had remembered to bring torches of their own—and a radio. Mr Pike shone his light from bed to bed and blanket to blanket. "Everybody here? Ready for sleep?"

164

I heard nineteen yeses. Everyone was being so obedient and quiet. I stretched out, exhausted. What a day!

And then . . .

"Mummy, Buddy kicked me!"

"Hey, that's *my* rucksack!"

"Shh, I want to sleep!"

The members of the BSC got to work. "Kids, come on now . . ."

Oh, well. It was nice to know, in the middle of one of the worst storms of all time, that some things hadn't changed.

20th CHAPTER

KAREN

THURSDAY

DEAR GRANNY AND GRANDAD,

WERE YOU EVER IN A HURRICANE? I WAS! ITS NAME WAS HURRICANE BILL. IT CAME THROUGH STONEY BROOK THIS MORNING (WHEN IT WAS STILL DARK). BUT I WAS AWAKE! BOY, WAS IT SCARY! BUT WE'RE ALL ALIVE. OUR HOUSE DIDN'T BLOW AWAY. NOW IT'S SUNNY. I HOPE WE GET ANOTHER HURRICANE SOMEDAY. MAYBE YOU COULD COME VISIT AND SEE IT.

LOVE, KAREN

You know what? I had a secret wish. My secret wish was that Hurricane Bill would pick up our house and take it to Nebraska. That is where Granny and Grandad live.

It would be like the opposite of *The Wizard of Oz*. We would start off in a colourful place, Stoneybrook. And we would end up on a farm.

And we would not have to pay for plane tickets.

Well, it didn't really happen like that.

The excitement started on Wednesday. That was when my stepsister, Kristy, called her mother to tell her about the hurricane.

Kristy's mother, Elizabeth is married to my Daddy. They live in this gigantic house. My brother Andrew and I live there, too, every other weekend. The rest of the time we live with Mummy and my stepfather, Seth. Our house (Mummy and Seth's) is little. But it's also in Stoneybrook.

Anyway, we were in the little house when Kristy phoned the big house. The reason I know was because Elizabeth called us afterwards. She said that Kristy said Hurricane Bill had hit Sea City. Everybody was leaving the beach houses. The Pikes and the Barretts and the girls in the Babysitters Club were going to drive to a motel for the night.

After the call, Andrew looked scared. He went to the living room window and stared outside. "Is this the hurricane?" he asked.

"No, darling," Mummy answered. "Not yet."

Not *yet*? I suppose that meant we were going to get it, too.

I stood near Andrew and looked outside. Rain was pouring down. The street was covered with water and tree branches. I couldn't imagine what a hurricane would look like. Poor Kristy.

The rest of the day I was dying to know what happened in Sea City. Did they find a place for all those people to stay in? Did the hurricane wreck any houses? Was anybody hurt?

I called Daddy's house after dinner, but the line was busy.

I called later and the line was still busy.

I called a third time and there was no answer.

I tried to call a fourth and fifth time, but there was not even a dialling tone.

I went into the study. Seth, Mummy, and Andrew were watching the TV news. "The phone is not working," I said.

Seth nodded. "The lines are down all over Stoneybrook."

Boo, boo, boo. How was I going to find out about Kristy?

I sat down between Seth and Mummy on the sofa. The newscasters were talking about damage to "coastal areas". We saw videos of smashed houses, waves crashing at people's front doors, cars up to their roofs in water, people rowing boats down *streets* covered with water.

"Is Sea City a coastal area?" I asked.

"Yes," Mummy replied.

"Did they say anything about it on the news?" I went on.

"They evacuated the beach," Seth answered. "That means everybody left their houses. Nobody's been hurt. That's the most important part. I'm sure Kristy is safe."

We watched some more. Then I asked, "Are *we* a coastal area?"

"Well, yes," Seth said.

"Does that mean Hurricane Bill is coming to Stoneybrook?"

Mummy put her arm around me. "Sometime late tonight or early tomorrow morning," she said. "If it stays on course."

"Oh."

"But we don't have a boat," Andrew said.

"We won't need one," Seth replied.

Andrew didn't seem convinced.

I don't know why I was not scared, but I wasn't. I was excited! I had never, ever been in a hurricane.

When an advert came on, Seth stood up and said, "We'd better start preparing for this."

Andrew and I followed him into the pantry. He found a big roll of masking tape. Then he went from window to window and put tape on them in this pattern:

I helped him. Soon Mummy came in and helped, too.

Then we were ready. We watched some more news. After that Andrew and I were allowed to watch a video, since we couldn't go outside.

Then it was bedtime. I said good night to everyone and lay down in my bed. I read a little. I looked out of the window. The rain was getting worse. The wind was howling.

Was *this* the hurricane?

I lay down again. I talked to Goosie a little (Goosie is my stuffed cat). I read some more. I thought about Kristy. I looked out of the window again.

I did not sleep. At least I do not think I did.

All I know is that when the tree fell a little way down the block, I heard it. It went *CRRRRRRACCKK*!

Then I heard Andrew scream. I ran into Mummy and Seth's room. Andrew was already in there, crying. "Is this it?" I asked.

"I think this may be it," Seth said.

170

We went downstairs to the kitchen. Seth turned on the radio. Mummy made some hot chocolate, even though it was summer.

"*Hurricane Bill is now sweeping through Stoneybrook,*" the radio man said. "*Fortunately at this hour, there are few if any people on the street. The telephone company is still working to restore lines, although that won't happen for at least another day. The fire department is standing by for emergencies, and a few crews are already clearing debris from the main arteries . . .*"

"Clearing the Brie from someone's arteries?" I said.

I thought Seth and Mummy were going to fall over laughing. "*Debris* is stuff that's blown into the street. And that's what they mean by arteries—streets."

"Oh."

I looked at the clock on the cooker and saw the time: 3:51. I couldn't believe it. I was staying up so late!

Our windows began to rattle like crazy. We looked between the strips of tape, but we couldn't even see across the street. The rain was like a curtain. And the street was a river. It wasn't deep enough for a rowing boat, though. (Boo.)

I don't know when I fell asleep. All I know is that when I woke up the next morning, I was in my bed.

And the sun was shining!

I looked outside. The front garden was a soggy mess. Branches were all over the place. Someone's postbox was in a puddle on the pavement. The surface of the street only showed through in the middle, because the gutters were full of water. A lorry with a crane was parked on the corner. The crane reached to the top of a telephone pole, where someone was busily working.

Seth and Mummy were outside with a few neighbours, cleaning up. I got dressed and ran out to help.

"I knew those trees would fall one day!" someone was saying. "When they put in the kerbs, they cut away the tree roots."

I looked down the street. There were three trees, small ones, that had fallen into the street. A fire engine was pulling up beside the farthest one.

"'Morning, sweetheart," Mummy said. "The storm is over. No one was hurt. We just have some fallen trees, and a few power lines are down."

"Well, there'll be plenty of wood for winter!" our neighbour said.

Mummy and Seth laughed. I looked up at the telephone repair person.

All I could think about was Kristy. I hoped she was all right.

21st CHAPTER

Buddy

Thusday

Dear Daddy,
Did you think the hericane got me? It didnt! Gues were we stayed? In a jim with a milion people. It was realy fun becase we had ice cream and the seeling did not leke. Now were back in are house and were CAMPING which is becase we have no elelctrisity!!!
What a GRAT HOLIDAY!!!!!!!!!!!!!!!!!!
Your pal
Buddy

173

Buddy

When I woke up, I forgot I was in the shelter. I thought I was at home. My bed at home is against the wall. So I rolled over and fell off the bed.

I landed on Mum.

"Aaaaah!" she screamed.

"Oh! Sorry!" I said.

Stacey woke up too, but Suzi and Marnie stayed asleep. So Stacey stayed with the Sleeping Uglies while Mum and I went to the canteen for breakfast. There was toast and jam. Also butter that was far too soft. And coffee. And fruit cocktail from big tins. But nothing else.

It was a pretty horrible breakfast.

Everybody woke up soon, even the Pikes. But I was the first one finished with breakfast. I ate three pieces of toast. I was still hungry, but I couldn't bear another piece.

Then the man with the megaphone came in and told us the sun was shining. We couldn't tell because of the boards covering the windows.

You should have heard the place. All these people clapped and cheered.

Soon Mum said, "Let's go before the rush."

We got out really fast, all twenty of us. Marnie stepped in a million puddles, but no one cared. When I did, Stacey and Mum yelled at me. Even though I was wearing my boots. That is so unfair.

We got in the car and drove to our house. It took SO LONG. I could have walked there faster.

174

As we drove along the main street, Mrs Pike said, "Looks like we were lucky."

I didn't think so. The Ferris wheel hadn't fallen down. The shop windows hadn't broken. No cars had crashed. No houses had blown away. No dead bodies were in the street. Nothing had happened.

It was *boring*.

When we reached the houses we saw *some* cool stuff. Tiles were missing on three roofs. A couple of houses did have broken windows, and someone's porch had collapsed.

Finally we got home. I wanted to play on the beach, until I got close to it.

What a disgusting mess. There were dead fish all over the place. Also soggy clothes and bottles and cans and rubbish. All the dustbins were missing. Stacey said the fish were probably using them underwater. She's funny sometimes, for a babysitter.

We went inside. Everything was exactly where we had left it. But guess what? We had no electricity, even after Mum turned it on. And when I went to get some water, the tap spat at me! Then *brown* liquid came out, like smelly prune juice.

I filled a cup and tried to give it to Suzi. She didn't think it was funny. And Mum and Stacey shouted at me again.

Soon we went over to the Pikes'. Margo and

175

Buddy

Vanessa told me we were going to go back to Stoneybrook. But they were lying.

Mr Pike said, "Hey, we've been through the worst. I think we can stick it out the rest of the way."

All of us kids said "Yeah!" So did the babysitters.

I thought Mum would want to go home, but even she wanted to stay. "It'll be fun," she said. "Having barbecues every day, reading by candlelight . . ."

So for two whole days, we had barbecue for breakfast, lunch, and dinner. Some neighbours started a group called Operation Recovery, and we joined in. I helped a *policeman* pick up rubbish on the beach! He called me Buddy, even though he didn't know that was my name. That happens sometimes.

At night, we lit candles and told ghost stories. Dawn came over one night and told this scary one about Jared Mullray's girlfriend—who may still be in Dawn's barn!

I was really sad on Friday night, because we had to leave on Saturday. I think Mum knew how I felt. When she blew out my candle, she sat on my bed and whispered, "Are you okay?"

"You know," I answered, "I was scared when Hurricane Bill came. But now I think it was the best thing about the holiday."

Mum laughed. "You were a great pioneer, Buddy."

"Yeah, like Davy Crockett."

Mum began to sing, "King of the Wild Frontierrrr . . ."

I love that song. We sang together. I started feeling better. Then I drifted to sleep.

You know what? I decided something that night.

My mum is cool.

22nd CHAPTER

LOGAN

FRIDAY

DEAR MARYANNE,

WELCOME HOME. AS I WRITE THIS, I
AM THINKING OF OUR NIGHT IN SEA CITY.
REMEMBER WHEN WE WENT INTO THE
HAUNTED HOUSE, AND THE LIGHTS WENT
OUT? I PULLED YOU CLOSE. YOU PUT
YOUR ARMS AROUND MY SHOULDER. WE
TURNED TO EACH OTHER AND STARTED
TO KISS.

IF THE ORANGE SLIME CREATURE
HADN'T POPPED OUT OF THE WALL, IT
WOULD HAVE BEEN A WONDERFUL
MOMENT.

OH WELL. JUST THINK. NOW WE
HAVE THE AUTUMN TO SEARCH

FOR EVEN MORE ROMANTIC MOMENTS.
SOUND LIKE A GOOD IDEA?

    I REALLY, REALLY MISSED YOU.
I HOPE YOU LIKE THE SURPRISE I
PLANNED.

               LOVE,
               YOUR HAPPY BOYFRIEND
                    LOGAN

"Hi, Terry, it's Logan," I said into the phone.

Terry is a new friend of mine. He's another waiter at the Rosebud Cafe. His parents run a big animal farm that's a tourist attraction in Mercer, Connecticut.

"Hi!" Terry said. "Listen, I talked to my dad about your idea for your girlfriend's welcome-home surprise."

"Yeah?"

"He wants to talk to you. I'll get him."

"Okay."

I waited patiently. It was Friday, and Mary Anne was coming back the next day. I wanted to do something really special for her.

I couldn't wait to see her. Especially after the week I'd had. It had been the absolute pits.

Why? Well, let me come right out and say it. From the moment I left Sea City, I couldn't stop thinking about Alex.

I know, I know. It sounds stupid, but there it is.

179

I had tried to put him out of my mind. I mean, he's just a *boy*. Just Mary Anne's friend.

But I kept thinking how much *free time* Mary Anne had in Sea City. Was she really going to want to spend it all with the same friends she saw every day in Stoneybrook? No way. I wouldn't if I were her.

On Monday and Tuesday nights, I kept imagining her and Alex on the Sea City boardwalk. Each night I had this urge to phone her— you know, just to say hi, how are you. But I thought I might sound suspicious (well, I *was*). And what if she were out? I'd feel *worse*.

So I didn't phone. Instead I just hoped she'd call me.

I didn't hear from her. Then on Wednesday everyone was talking about Hurricane Bill. I began to feel really worried. I tried to call the Pikes' house, but no one answered.

I was going to try again on Thursday, but that was when the storm hit *us*. Our phone lines went dead.

When I finally got a dialling tone, I called the operator, "Hello? Yes, I'm trying to reach Sea City. . . . No, *Sea* City. Pardon? Service is still out? Okay, thank you."

"No luck?" Mum asked me.

"No," I replied glumly.

"Cheer up," Dad said. "The storm wasn't

nearly as bad as they thought it would be. I'm sure they'll be okay."

"Yeah."

I knew Mary Anne was still there. If she'd escaped, she would have phoned immediately. The last postcard I'd received from her was dated Tuesday. She'd mentioned the storm at the very end, after a little section about Alex and Toby.

I thought they must be on the island, too.

Great.

I kept trying to be realistic. There were probably a lot of people there. I tried to imagine where they would be. I had heard the houses were evacuated, and the electricity was out. People were probably huddled together somewhere. Maybe in one of the boardwalk shops. Maybe on the Ghost Train.

I was *sure* Alex was with the Pikes. In a crisis, people always stick with other people they know.

I could just see it. No lights, everyone pulling together, singing songs and making the best of it. People arm in arm. Like a scene from a film.

And in a dimly lit corner sit the hero and heroine. They hold hands and vow to brave it together. Then, as the singing swells and the candlelight flickers, they lean towards each other. . . .

Bruno, get a grip, I told myself.

At 9:45, the phone rang. "I'll get it!" I shouted.

181

I ran into the kitchen and picked it up. "Hello!"

"Hello, Logan? Ohhhhh, it's so good to hear your voice. What a week! How are you?"

I was ecstatic. I was relieved. I was angry. I was hurt. So many complicated thoughts were running around in my head. But the only word I could manage was "Mary Anne?"

"Yes! Can you hear me okay?" she asked loudly.

"Fine!" I said. "Where are you?"

"Still in Sea City. Oh, I have so much to tell you when I get back. Guess what? They've fixed the causeway a few hours ago."

"Wow, so you're going to come home—?"

"Tomorrow, just the way we planned."

"That's great!" I said. "But—but how is everyone? No one got hurt?"

"No. Everyone's fine. I mean, the storm was scary. But we've had the *best* time!"

"And all your neighbours and friends? You know, Toby and Alex, for instance."

Ugh. Very subtle, Bruno.

"They're fine. We saw them today for the first time all week. They spent the storm inland. Their cars were the last ones to make it over the causeway before the flood."

"Oh," I said. "Hmm, how lucky. . . ."

Whoa. Did I feel stupid. Idiotic. Off the scale on the Dorkometer.

I was glad Mary Anne could not see the colour of my face.

One whole week of guessing and second-guessing. Worrying and suspecting and assuming. I suppose I *should* have felt ecstatic. (Well, I did, sort of.) But it was almost a letdown. I mean, all that worrying had been a lot of work—and for nothing!

We had a great phone call. I didn't mention a word about how I'd felt. I just let myself steep in guilt, like a tea bag.

That was when I had the urge to give Mary Anne something really special as a welcome-home present. And Terry Dutton's dad came to mind.

So that brings me to Friday. There I was, waiting for Terry's dad to come on the phone.

"Hi, are you Terry's friend?" he asked.

"Yes, sir," I said.

"What's this idea Terry tells me about?"

I described my plan to him. It was a little wacky, and I thought he'd say no.

He listened to every word, and then said, "Young man, that is the craziest idea I ever heard—"

"I'm sorry to take up your time, sir," I cut in. "Thank you for—"

"And I love it!" he continued. "Sounds like the kind of thing I used to do with Terry's mum when we were young."

183

"R-really?" I said.

"You don't think we had any spunk when we were young?"

"No! I mean, yes! I mean, I'm sure you did. It's just—"

He laughed. "All right, Logan. Let's decide a time of delivery and return, and I'll take care of the rest."

I couldn't believe he had said yes. Mary Anne was going to be thrilled out of her mind!

23rd CHAPTER

Mallory

Dear Diary,

Did I make the right decision? I think so.
When I look back and read this, I will say,
"Mallory Pike, you showed courage and
maturity."

Either that or, "Whoa, were you out of
your mind?"

No, I doubt that.

Let me start at the beginning.

Today was my Big Date with Toby....

185

Mallory

My heart was fluttering the minute I woke up. I threw aside my covers. I ran to the mirror.

Left side of face. Right side of face. No pimples. Good.

It hadn't been a great summer, blemishwise. When you're as fair as I am, your skin can do weird things in the heat. Blisters, pimples, heat rashes, you name it.

But not this morning. Not the morning of the evening of the Big Date.

Okay. Hair. Horrendous as usual. Thick and frizzy and piled up on one side from sleeping. A cross between Bozo the Clown and the Bride of Frankenstein (Frankenstein the Clown? The Bride of Bozo?) But I could cope with that.

I found my brush and did my ritual morning arm-wrestle with my hair. I managed to control it enough to trap it with some hair clips.

Then I pinched my cheeks, said, "Good morning, beautiful," and went downstairs.

This was not like me.

In case you haven't noticed, I am not Miss Fashion-and-Glamour of the Babysitters Club. (More like Miss Brace-and-Glasses.) But I was meeting *him* tonight.

What would I wear? Should I put on make-up? Could I learn *how* to put on make-up in time? Should I practise what to say? Should I leave my glasses at home?

186

I was beginning to realize what it must be like to be Stacey.

Uh, no. *Not* a good comparison. For one thing, I wasn't feeling mean and jealous.

Which was how Stacey had been acting for days. She had hardly said a word to me. When she did, she made sure it was something nasty.

At first I felt confused and hurt. But not any more. By Friday I was determined to have a fun, relaxing day.

If I could keep myself from exploding with anticipation.

So I bounced downstairs and cried, "Good morning!"

As usual, Jessi was already up, making pancakes and eggs and bacon.

"Listen, Mallory!" Adam exclaimed. He was grinning broadly. "I one my mother . . . I two my mother . . . I three my mother . . . I four my mother . . . I five my mother . . ."

My siblings were chanting along with him now. I could see where this was leading.

"I six my mother . . . I seven my mother . . . I EIGHT MY MOTHER!"

They erupted with laughter. "Get it?" Adam said. "I *ate* my mother!"

I tried very hard not to laugh. It would only encourage him. "Adam, eat your pancakes," I replied.

When the kids had finished, my friends and I

sat down to breakfast. "Are you ready?" Jessi asked me with a sly grin.

"Actually," I said, "I was thinking of going into town to get some hair slides, maybe a fun kind of . . . badge?"

"I'll go with you!" Claudia volunteered.

"Me too!" Jessi said.

"Don't worry about the kids," Mary Anne added. "We'll take care of them."

What great friends. "Okay!" I said. "Thanks!"

Well, Claudia and Jessi and I had the best time. Claudia found me a pair of hairslides in the shape of flamingoes—but cool, not corny-looking. Then we bought about ten tiny badges with pictures on them. The faces included Virginia Woolf, Jimi Hendrix, Stephen Hawking, and Janis Joplin, but Claud didn't know who any of them were. She just picked them because they looked "funky".

On the way back, guess who we ran into?

Stacey was taking the Barrett kids to the boardwalk for ice cream. "Hi," she said.

"Hi," Jessi and Claudia answered.

"Where've you been?" Stacey asked.

"Shopping," I said, clutching my bag a little tighter.

"Ooh, can I see?"

I felt awkward. I didn't want to be rude, so I opened the bag for her.

"Wow . . . really *interesting*," Stacey said. "Is this stuff for Margo and Vanessa?"

"No," I replied, grabbing the bag back. "It happens to be for me."

"Well, ex*cuuuuse* me," Stacey shot back. She began shoving the Barrett kids ahead of her. "I suppose we'll see you later."

When we were far enough away, I said, "See? She hates me."

Jessi sighed and shook her head. "I just don't understand what's going on between you two."

We walked back to the house. "Claudia," I said, "do you think I should wear jeans and a T-shirt with this stuff, or something fancier?"

"Show me what you have," Claudia replied, "and we'll work something out."

The three of us ran inside and upstairs. We pulled out just about every outfit I had brought.

Claudia took a look at everything. Then she made Jessi take out *her* outfits.

I tried on casual. I tried on smart. I tried on weird combinations. I just followed the directions of Claudia Kishi, Fashion Consultant.

As I slipped on a clingy, short sundress, I heard high-pitched squeaks behind me.

Mice? No, Pikes.

Jessi opened the door. Adam, Jordan, and Nicky fell into the room. "Hrrrrrumph!" Jessi said.

They scrambled to their feet. "Oh, um, we

189

were—ha ha—looking for Nicky's Etch-a-Sketch," Adam said.

Claudia glanced around. "Hmmm, doesn't seem to be here in Jessi and Mal's room."

"Okay, 'bye!" The boys were off like a shot. We could hear them giggling as they ran down the stairs. Then: "Mal and Toby sitting in a tree, N-E-C-K-I-N-G!"

"*Boys*!" my dad's voice bellowed.

"Now, where were we?" Claudia said.

We worked for another half an hour. I ended up choosing a short, flared, white-on-blue polka-dotted skirt (mine); a white, ribbed tank-top (Jessi's); and a long, royal-blue men's shirt with the tails tied in front (Claudia had run to *her* room for that). Claudia insisted I didn't wear anything too light or it would "wash out my face." We carefully placed some of the badges we'd bought on the tank-top.

Claudia yanked back my mane and worked out how to put the flamingo hairslides in it so they wouldn't get lost.

I looked in the mirror. I watched a smile light up my face. "Wow! I look pretty good."

"Pretty good?" Claudia repeated. "You look *sensational*! Toby's eyes are going to fall out!"

"That ought to be an interesting date," Jessi remarked.

I sighed. "Doesn't this remind you of the time you helped me dress for the Valentine Dance?"

Claudia laughed. "After you'd had that big fight with Ben—over how to use the *library card catalogue*?"

Ben.

I really hadn't thought of him. Ben Hobart was the only boy I ever went out with before this trip. We'd been to the cinema, and just about all of the school dances. I'd never officially called him my boyfriend or anything, though.

So why was I feeling this sudden twinge of guilt?

"Remember when you went to the cinema with the little cafe?" Jessi asked.

I cringed. "And I poured sugar on the popcorn!"

We laughed. And I felt this incredible urge to call Ben. I really *missed* him.

I put aside my outfit and changed into beach clothes. Then I told Jessi and Claudia I'd meet them outside, and I went into my parents' room.

I still remembered Ben's number.

"Hello, Hobart residence."

Mr Hobart's voice made me break into a smile. The Hobarts are from Australia and speak with this wonderful accent. "Hi, Mr Hobart! This is Mallory!"

"Well, hello, love! Let me get Ben for you!"

In a second, Ben was on the phone. "Hi, Mallory!"

Hoi, Mel-ry! Oh, was that great! He sounded thrilled. "Hi, Ben. How are you?"

"Alive." *Aloiv*. "I guess you survived the storm, huh? We lost a tree. It missed our car by about five inches!"

We talked and talked and talked. We didn't stop until we'd filled in the past two weeks. I found out that Johnny Hobart had switched on all the torches the night before the storm "to warm them up." Of course, their block was the only one to lose power in the hurricane. Then Ben told me how Mathew tried to grab "a cocoon" in the branch of the tree that fell in the street—and it turned out to be a sleeping bat.

It was the funniest, happiest conversation I'd had in a long time. I didn't want to hang up.

When I did, I realized something.

There was no one I wanted to go out with but Ben.

I tried to get excited about my date with Toby again. But I just couldn't. The thrill was competely gone.

I walked slowly downstairs, in a daze. Then I went to the beach and spent the rest of the afternoon with everyone. Later I talked to Jessi about it.

"Look," she said, "it's up to you. What time is he picking you up?"

"Seven o'clock."

Jessi looked at her watch. "You have an hour.

This is your last day in Sea City. Do whatever makes you happy."

"But my mind is so mixed up," I said.

"Well, don't do it from your mind, then. Do it from your heart."

I giggled. "Jessi, that's corny."

She laughed, too. "It's true, though."

Jessi is so clever.

The beach was starting to get that cool, late afternoon feeling. All the Pikes and Barretts were playing extra hard, building extra nice castles, taking extra long swims.

I was going to miss this place so much. Maybe it would be best just to spend the last day with my friends and family.

"You decided not to go on your date?"

Trust Stacey McGill to destroy a wonderful mood.

I turned to look at her. "I didn't say that."

Stacey shrugged. "Sorry. It was just getting late. I thought maybe you'd come to your senses."

That did it.

"For your information, I *am* going. In fact, I was just heading back to the house now."

I stormed away. There was no way I'd give Stacey the satisfaction of thinking she changed my mind!

I marched straight to my room and put on my outfit. Then I waited on the porch, pacing back and forth.

193

Mallory

Toby arrived at seven. He was smiling as he walked to the porch. And he looked gorgeous.

But the side of me that wanted to go was saying: *Stacey will be so jealous*. And the rest of me was saying, *I wish Ben were here*.

"You look great, cutie!" Toby said, stepping onto the porch.

I smiled. I looked him in the eye.

Do it from the heart, Jessi had said. Somehow, that silly little statement made things much clearer.

"Toby," I said. "Um, I feel really embarrassed about something. Can we . . . uh, talk?"

He shrugged. "We are talking."

Go for it, I told myself. "Toby, I know I should have said this earlier, but I have this boyfriend at home. His name is Ben, and . . . well, we're kind of going steady."

Toby's smile disappeared. "Oh. Well, I didn't know. . . ."

"You couldn't have. I'm really sorry. You came all the way over here and everything. But, I suppose I was just so *amazed* you'd even be interested in me. I mean, you're a really nice boy and all . . ."

"I can't convince you to go out just as a friend?"

I shook my head. "It's my family's last evening here. I think I'm going to spend it with them."

Toby sighed and looked down. "Well, I think I

understand. I mean, if I had a steady girl I'd do the same."

"Thanks," I said.

Toby forced a smile. "Well, have a fun time. If you come back next summer and know of another cute girl who's unattached, let me know, okay?"

Huh?

"Okay," I said. "'Bye, Toby."

"'Bye, Mal."

I went back into the house to change. I dragged myself up the stairs. Walking down the hall to my room, I was lost in thought. I had ruined Toby's night, and that didn't seem fair. But that *comment* he made! Was that all I was to him, just "another cute girl"?

I flung open my door.

Stacey was sitting on the bed.

I stared at her. "For your information, Toby did not dump me," I said. "That's not why I'm back so soon."

Stacey looked as if she were about to cry. "Oh, Mallory, I'm sorry . . . about everything."

All my anger melted away. Stacey stood up, and we gave each other a big, big hug. "It's okay," I said.

"No, it's not," Stacey replied. "I was a jerk. For some reason, I was jealous that Toby liked *you*, when he had dumped *me*. I just talked to Jessi about it. I—I don't want to be enemies. A boy isn't worth that. You can do whatever you want."

"I already have," I said. "And I'll tell you about it at the barbecue tonight."

"You—you're staying?"

I nodded. "But not looking like this. Mind if I change?"

For the first time in two weeks, I saw a smile cross Stacey's face.

I took the flamingoes from my hair and started thinking about spare ribs. This was my last night in Sea City, and I planned to have some *fun*!

EPILOGUE

Dear Alex,
You know what
was waiting for me
at the Pikes' house
when we got home?
A horse and cart.
A real one! Logan
had <u>hired</u> it to
take me home!!
Oh, I thought I
was going to pass out.
It was so romantic.
We threw my luggage
in and clopped down
the street. The Pikes,
the Barretts, and my
friends all cheered as
we rode away.

197

Logan's friend
Terry was the driver,
and he kept trying
to tell jokes. But I
didn't mind a bit.
 I will never forget
this my whole life.
 Sincerely,
 Mary Anne
P.S. How was your
 trip back?
P.P.S. Good luck with
 baseball season,
 whenever it starts.

Hi daddy,
 Were back and its much
more boring here. Nicky
did not thro up on the way
back. Mumy and stacy had
a long talk and mum kept
sayig she was sory about
somthing i dont kno what.
But they were cereus for a
long time and then real
freindly. We playd lots of
gams untill Marny becam a
pan in the you kno what.
 WRIGHT BACK!!!!!!!!!!!!
 Buddy

Dear Dad,

How was the hurricane in the Big Apple? Did any skyscrapers blow away? We all survived. Details when I see you this weekend.

Remember I told you about Toby, that boy who dumped me? Well, he tried to pick up Mallory Pike. Yes, Mallory Pike. She fell for him at first, but then decided to remain true to Ben Hobart. I was really proud of her. I was thinking of inviting her along when I come to New York. Would it be OK?

Luv, Stace

FIRST GLASS, INC.
GLAZIERS & WINDOW DESIGN

Mr and Mrs Pike
10 Slate Street
Stoneybrook, CT
Dear Mr and Mrs Pike,
This is to confirm our appointment
for this Saturday at 10:00 A.M. for
the replacement of two (2) broken

199

living room windows, one (1) basement window, and one (1) bedroom window. Due to the unexpected extent of
storm damage to glass in your neighbourhood, we were unable to make the
appointment at an earlier date.

Sincerely,

Robert Thompson
Robert Thompson
Manager

Dear Kristy,
We are still on
holiday don't kick
us of the team ok.
We still want to play.
even if the other
players you got were
realy good.
From,
Jake Kuhn

Hi, Claudia!
Are you home yet? What a summer you must have had! I heard about Hurricane Bill. We missed it completely up here.
So, now that you're all home with nothing to do for a couple of weeks, how about a BSC trip to see a fellow member in Oklahoma?
Maybe you could come with the Pikes and the Barretts?
Oh, well, think about it.
Love, Shannon

ELLEN COOKE AGENCY
Beachfront Property

Dear Pike Family,
Thank you so much for your good nature and perseverence during our weather emergency. You took wonderful care of the house, and damage was negligible. Other clients were not so lucky (*I* was not so lucky in some cases).

201

I will be happy to hold the house open
for you next summer. I'm sure it will
be a sunny, perfect August!

Sincerely,

Ellen Cooke

Ellen Cooke

Dear Mallory,
   I just want you to
know, I'm not angry with
you at all. In fact,
I'm kind of glad you
did what you did. If
you hadn't, it would
have been an
uncomfortable date.
   You have a steady
boyfriend and that's
cool. So maybe you
wouldn't mind sending
me the address of
your friend Jessi?
She seemed very
nice. How old is she?
Is she seeing some-
one?
   Hope to hear soon.
                    Toby